PHOENIX RISING

Karen Hesse

PUFFIN BOOKS

The author wishes to thank Charles Butterfield, Eileen Christelow, Eileen Houston, Liza Ketchum, Sarah Liston, Winifred Bruce Luhrmann, Deb Luskin, Robert MacLean, Cynthia Major, David Major, and Tim Shafer for their insightful counsel.

Heartfelt gratitude is extended to Brenda Bowen, Donna Bray, Barbara Kouts, my daughters Kate and Rachel, and most particularly to my husband, Randy Hesse.

PUFFIN BOOKS
Published by the Penguin Group
Penguin Putnam Inc., 345 Hudson Street, New York, New York 10014, U.S.A.
Penguin Books Ltd, 27 Wrights Lane, London W8 5TZ, England
Penguin Books Australia Ltd, Ringwood, Victoria, Australia
Penguin Books Canada Ltd, 10 Alcorn Avenue, Toronto, Ontario, Canada M4V 3B2
Penguin Books (N.Z.) Ltd, 182–190 Wairau Road, Auckland 10, New Zealand

Penguin Books Ltd, Registered Offices: Harmondsworth, Middlesex, England

First published in the United States of America by Henry Holt & Company, Inc., 1994
R printed by arrangement with Henry Holt & Company, Inc.
Published in Puffin Books, 1995

20 19 18 17

LIBRARY OF CONGRESS CATALOGING-IN-PUBLICATION DATA
Hesse, Karen.
Phoenix rising / Karen Hesse.
p. cm.
Summary: Thirteen-year-old Nye learns about relationships and death when fifteen-year-old Ezra, who was exposed to radiation leaked from a nearby nuclear plant, comes to stay at her grandmother's Vermont farmhouse.
ISBN 0-14-037628-3
[1. Nuclear power plants—Accidents—Fiction. 2. Death—Fiction.
3. Friendship—Fiction.] I. Title.
PZ7.H4364Ph 1995 [Fic]—dc20 95-9432 CIP AC

Printed in the United States of America

For the children of Three Mile Island.
For the children of Chernobyl.
For all of us, children of a nuclear age.

"Look not back in anger, nor forward in fear—but around you in awareness."

—Ross Hersey

Phoenix Rising

 \ *One*

Snapping my arm forward, I winged a stone toward the woods. It fell short of Ripley Powers's dog, Tyrus. I meant it to fall short. I had no wish to hurt the dog, only to chase him off.

"Get on home!" I yelled through the gauze mask that had covered my face for nearly a week now. I shook my fist at the dog. "Get on home, Tyrus!"

Even after he'd run into the woods, Tyrus's barking cut through the crisp November air, echoing down the valley.

Back across the field, in a corner of the front pasture, the yearling sheep crowded together, except for one, lying alone on the cold ground. I studied it from the road, waiting for some sign of movement. I saw none.

Brushing my hair back with the crook of my arm, I scowled. "Damn dog."

Muncie stood beside me. "It's Ripley's fault, letting Tyrus run loose."

Ripley's dog took off running every chance he got. If he couldn't find any trouble on our farm, he'd go agitating somewhere else. One time Red Jackson picked Tyrus up all the way to Cookshire, over the mountains and forty miles south of here. That was when there still was a Cookshire.

Dropping her backpack beside mine, Muncie crunched after me across the brittle November grass. Her short, bowed legs struggled against the pitch of the land.

Long-legging it over the electric fence, I got inside with the yearlings.

Muncie stayed outside in the field.

As I approached the fallen ewe, the rest of the flock pressed tighter toward the far fence. Their steamy breath came fast, forming a cloud over their heads.

I knelt before the bloody sheep, my mind racing. Radiation scared me most. That was everyone's fear these days.

But I'd lived on a sheep farm long enough to know radiation hadn't killed this ewe. Her rear end, her throat, her insides, were torn open. My mask puffed in and out; a nettle of anger stung at my chest.

We had just let this flock out of the barn yesterday, even though radiation was still leaking down at Cookshire.

So much time spent worrying about overcrowding the sheep in the barn to protect them from fallout. We never considered a dog attack.

"Nyle?" Muncie asked. "Is the sheep dead?"

"Ayuh."

"What killed it?"

As much as I worried about radiation, Muncie and her family feared it ten times worse. We'd all hovered over our radios, listening to the reports since last week. The announcers assured us of our safety. And we all wanted to believe them. But dread wore the Harrises to the bone. They feared more for Muncie, because of her being a runt to begin with.

"Tyrus killed the sheep," I told Muncie. "Just Tyrus."

Turning away from the kill, I stood, my fists clenched, looking across the field toward the Powers property.

I heard Ripley coming before I saw him. He was yelling at his dog. That boy always yelled. Seems like he didn't know any other way of talking.

Ripley appeared through a break in the trees, looking huge, even for a fifteen-year-old. He stood on the tangled bank at the edge of his property, his legs wide apart in the weedy grass. Tyrus, with a blood-stained muzzle, fawned around Ripley's feet.

Ripley's radiation mask stretched up around his forehead. He was the only one I knew who refused to wear his mask all the time. Looking over at me and Muncie, Ripley folded his long arms across his chest.

"Tyrus kill one of your sheep?" he yelled.

"Damn right he did."

"Why don't you get yourself another guard dog?"

"Why don't you tie *your* dog up?" My grip tightened on the bony handles of my hips.

Ripley glared at me from across the road. Even from this distance, I could make out the droop of the lid over his bad eye. He reached up, rubbing where the mask cut into the back of his neck.

"I wish that mask would strangle him," I mumbled. "I swear, I do."

"Nyle." Muncie's voice warned me to cool down.

Muncie was right. A thirteen-year-old girl, even one as thorny as I was, had no place messing with the likes of Ripley

Powers. He was too big, too strong.

But I couldn't help it. That boy sent the blood swarming in my head.

Ripley took a half step forward and tugged off his mask. He tossed the wad of gauze down the bank, into the road.

Looked like he meant to start some kind of trouble. I whistled for my dog, Caleb. Caleb's a Border collie, a herding dog, low and fast, silky black and white. With Ripley looking so threatening, I would have felt better having Caleb nearby. But he didn't come to my whistle. Must have been inside with Gran.

All I had standing beside me was Muncie. The November sun shone on Muncie Harris's straw-blond hair, the way it shines on a cabbage in the kitchen garden. She stood on her short legs, breathing hard through her radiation mask.

"Forget about Ripley," she said. "You'd better tell your grandmother about that dead ewe. She'll want to call Red Jackson right away."

Every year at town meeting the people of North Haversham elected Red Jackson as town officer. He's the one got us radiation detectors and masks after the accident.

Whenever we had a sheep kill, Red would come out to the farm, take a look at the evidence. If a dog, and not some coyote, had done the killing, the town paid us for our loss. Usually dogs went for the rear first, coyotes for the throat. Considering the condition of the sheep and the bloody mess on Tyrus's face, the dog's guilt would not be hard to prove.

I high-stepped back over the fence, out of the pasture, to stand beside Muncie. Ripley scowled across the field at us.

"Hey, Munchkin, grown any brains yet? Maybe with all this radiation in the air, you'll mutate into something normal."

I started toward him in anger but Muncie held me back.

"How much is two plus two, Munchkin?" Ripley yelled.

Muncie shifted on the uneven, tufted grass, staying me with her iron grip. I jerked my arm away, causing her to lose her balance. Muncie stumbled backward into the electric fence. Her hand brushed the hot wire.

She jumped at the sting.

Laughing, Ripley pointed at her. "Nyle Sumner, why do you hang around with that dwarf?"

The way he said it made it sound ugly.

I turned my back on him.

"Are you okay?" I asked.

Muncie tucked her right arm tight against her chest. Tears stood in her pale eyes, magnified by her glasses.

"I'm going to kill him. Just walk over there and kill him," I said, twisting around to face Ripley again.

"No, Nyle," Muncie whispered, coming up close to me. She cradled her shocked arm.

Ripley shifted a big wad of spit in his mouth and hurled it. It arched and landed in the dirt road between us. I took another step forward. Muncie's left hand reached out, this time to hold me back.

Just then Ripley's dog caught the scent of something behind him in the woods. He backed up, lifted his head, and started baying. Turning tail, he took off, vanishing between the trees. Ripley, yelling for Tyrus to come back, stomped off after him.

Anger rose up in me like spring sap. I marched toward the road, meaning to cross over.

"Forget it, Nyle."

Muncie struggled behind me, rocking on her short legs

over the treacherous, sloping ground.

"You can't fight Ripley, Nyle. No one can. Forget it."

I swung around to face her. "I could—"

"He's fifteen! And twice your weight. And besides, he's a boy."

"I could fight him."

I stopped in the road to pick up the backpack I'd dropped minutes earlier. I stared at the place where Ripley and Tyrus had stood.

"This makes half a dozen sheep we've lost in one year to that dog." I beat road dust off my backpack.

"At least he killed only one this time," Muncie said.

Last May, Ripley's dog slaughtered five of our sheep in one night. That was after Birch, our old guard dog, had died.

"Tyrus won't kill any more of your sheep," Muncie said. "Red Jackson'll see to that. Come on, Nyle. Let's get home."

As we climbed the steep road, sloping pasture to one side, Ripley's woods to the other, I slowed way down, matching my pace to Muncie's. We didn't even try talking. Climbing pinched the breath right out of her.

We stopped at the fork that led to my house. Muncie's chest worked hard, trying to suck enough air in.

"Are you—coming up—to do homework?"

I usually did after chores, but Gran would need help burying the sheep. Damn that Tyrus.

"I don't know if I'll make it tonight. Probably not."

"Nyle," Muncie urged. "Whatever you do, don't mess with Ripley."

"I will if I want." But my temper had cooled some.

"You don't have to go around with me," Muncie said. "Not if it causes trouble."

I liked Muncie. Nobody else ever bothered getting to know her. They just looked at her big head, her short arms and legs, and thought they knew everything about her. Sometimes people were mean, like Ripley. I never heard her complain, though it must have galled her.

"I don't know how you stand by and suffer Ripley's insults," I said.

Behind her glasses, she lowered her blue eyes. "I just do."

I gazed over the rolling autumn fields, speckled with sheep. The mountains rose gently on either side of the valley.

"Ripley can't tell me who to be friends with," I said. "I choose my own friends. I don't give a skunk's turd what he thinks."

Muncie nodded.

After she got her wind back, she continued up the hill. Her parents rented one of Gran's houses, the one high above the back pasture, at the edge of the upper woodlot.

I waited until she waved the all clear. Then I started down my drive, hurrying to get inside and tell Gran about the sheep.

But as I passed the corner of the farmhouse, I stopped. Something was different.

It was the curtain. The curtain to the back bedroom was closed.

We never closed that curtain, not even last week, right after the accident. We'd shut off the whole house and spent most of our time in the basement, but we hadn't shut that curtain.

On a normal day I walked past the back bedroom at least

a dozen times. The curtain was never drawn. But now it hung across the window, thick and heavy, a nasty shade of green, like a four-day-old bruise.

In our house, that bedroom was the dying room. My mother died there when I was six. And two years ago my grandfather died there. I hated that room.

Backing away from the window, I turned to fill the log carrier with firewood from the shed. Humping the wood across the driveway, I banged on the kitchen door with my elbow. Gran didn't come to meet me the way she usually did.

I waited, banged again.

Then, shifting my load, I freed my fingers, twisted the doorknob, and let myself in.

 *Two*

      I dragged the loaded carrier across the kitchen and dropped the logs into the wood box. They made a clatter like bowling pins and kicked up a cloud of dust. A couple of wood chips skittered across the linoleum floor. I kicked them back under the wood box with my boot.

"Gran?" Lifting the radiation detector from the kitchen table, I swept it across the room. The same level we'd registered all week. Eight days since the accident and always the steady click of a normal reading.

Pulling off my mask, I hung it on a hook by the stove. Mr. Perry, our principal, said as long as the wind kept blowing radiation away from us, we only needed our masks outside. Muncie's mother made Muncie wear her mask all the time.

"Gran?" I called again, looking through the doorway to her room. Her radio played softly. Since the accident, her radio played all the time as we listened for reports.

Usually Gran had a snack waiting for me. She'd keep me company while I ate, before we started afternoon chores. Caleb would doze on the hearth, resting up from morning. Bayley, my black-and-white cat, would curl on the chair nearest the stove. They were all missing.

"Caleb! Bayley! Gran!" I called, thinking about the curtain drawn in the back bedroom, trying to keep the worry out of my voice.

I opened the refrigerator; found half a pot of greasy, cold soup. I wasn't eating that.

"Gran! Caleb!"

I heard movement in the hallway. Soft movement. Something coming my way from the back bedroom.

Caleb appeared, prancing into the kitchen. His nails clicked as he hit the linoleum. He came around the table and stuck his nose into my palm, snuffling me.

"Where have you been, boy?" I asked. "What's going on down there?"

Placing his paws on my thigh, he thrust his head forward.

"You want some scratching?"

He leaned against me, tail high and wagging. But when I stopped, Caleb got down and pranced back toward the hall again. His feathery tail wagged behind him until he disappeared.

"Gran?" I called.

Part of me wanted to march down that hall after Caleb, but I stayed in the kitchen. I'd had too many bad dreams about that back bedroom. It had grown too black and hungry. I was never eager to go in there. Especially not now, with the curtain drawn.

The house smelled of one-pot stew. Normally the odor

of it carved my stomach hollow. During cold weather all Gran's meals were one-pot something, simmered all day on the woodstove.

I lifted the lid of the cast-iron kettle and thick, meaty steam rose into my nostrils. A stream of condensed moisture rained from the heavy lid, hitting the stove top and hissing. Reaching for Gran's blue spoon, I stirred the stew, turning chunks of potatoes, onions, carrots.

The whole mess needed more heat. I opened the stove door and used the blackened poker to spread the embers. Reaching into the wood box, I pulled out a couple splintery pieces of wood and laid them on the coals.

"Nyle."

Gran's voice rasped behind me. I hadn't heard her come up.

Crouching a few more seconds in front of the woodstove, I dared not show my relief at hearing her voice. The heat from the orange coals toasted my face.

Finally I stood. "Tyrus killed one of the yearlings in the front pasture," I said, turning to face her.

"Damn dog," Gran said. "I'll try to get through to Red. You put your things away upstairs, but come right back down, Nyle."

"Why?"

"I'll tell you when you get here."

"Tell me now."

Gran stood solid in front of me. "We're having those evacuees from the accident staying here after all."

Gran and I had discussed the possibility a couple days before.

"I thought we'd decided not to."

"I changed my mind," Gran said.

Well, I hadn't changed mine.

"Where are they staying?" I asked. "In the back bedroom?"

Gran nodded, picking up the phone.

My heart beat a little too fast, a little too high in my throat as I climbed the narrow steps from the kitchen to my room. I shrugged my backpack from my shoulder, dropping it on the window seat.

As I clicked on my radio, I heard Gran on the phone downstairs, trying to get through to Red Jackson. Since the accident, getting calls out took time. You used the phone for emergencies, nothing else.

Bayley snored softly in the center of my bed. I stretched across the quilt, scooped him into my arms, and scratched under his chin. His head tilted back, his eyes glazed, his purr sent a rumble of warmth through my bones.

Sitting on the edge of the high bed, Bayley in my lap, I listened to the radio. Nothing much new, but I had this need to stay and listen anyway.

North Haversham registered normal amounts of radiation, but just twenty miles east of here the level of fallout soared. Aunt May and Uncle Lemmy's entire herd of cattle had sickened. And my little cousin Bethany. She had sickened too.

As I sat listening, stroking Bayley, I heard Gran climbing the narrow stairs.

"I was coming down," I said.

Gran walked across the wood floor of the attic room and sat on my window seat. Her brown gaze never left my face.

We listened to the radio together. Bayley purred and licked my index finger over and over, softening me the way he did mice. Every now and then he'd close his teeth on my skin, but never hard enough to hurt.

Gran pushed at the net snugged around the edges of her dark hair as the news report continued.

I studied my grandmother, sitting on the window seat, her face round and wrinkled as a walnut. The radio crackled on my nightstand as a report came in from surveillance helicopters passing near the plume path.

"You think it will ever end?" I asked when the radio finally returned to music.

Gran shook her head. "Not for a long time."

"Gran, did you ever feel so angry you could see the blood inside your eyes?"

"You angry because of the accident, Nyle?"

I nodded. "That. And other things."

"That kind of anger's not good for you."

I turned off the radio. "I know."

"Let it go, Nyle. Come on down and eat something."

I eased Bayley back into the center of the quilt and smoothed the black fur on his side. Gran led the way down the stairs.

She went slowly. The dim light in the stairwell cast deep shadows, making it hard to see where one step ended and the next began. Gran turned to the side, gripped the worn rail, took one step at a time.

I could take the stairs with my eyes closed. I knew the landscape of each tread, the feel of the walls where my hands touched on the way down.

In the kitchen Gran sliced a piece of apple pie and a

wedge of cheese. She slid the snack in front of me on the old brown speckled china.

"I'll talk while you eat," Gran said in her husky voice.

I looked toward the hallway. "Is Caleb still down there?"

Gran said, "Eat, Nyle."

I dug my fork into the deep layers of crust and apple, breathing in the cinnamon smell.

"We'll be keeping those two evacuees here for a while," Gran said. "I picked them up at the hospital today. They're locals. Right from the south side of Cookshire. A woman, Miriam Trent, and her son, Ezra."

I pierced an apple slice with my fork.

"They've had a bad time," Gran said. "They lived close to the plant. The husband got a call the night of the accident and went straight over. Later, when the sirens went off, the boy tried reaching him. He took a lot of radiation."

"Gran, I don't want to know," I said.

Gran ignored me. "The boy's not too sick right now, but he was worse before and they say he'll get worse again."

"Can we catch it?"

"No, it's like your cousin Bethany. It's not contagious."

"If he's going to get so sick, why don't they keep him at the hospital?" He might live if he stayed at the hospital.

"There's already too many at the hospitals," Gran said. "Aunt May had to bring Bethany home too. You've heard the news reports."

I nodded, breaking my pie into small pieces, my appetite gone. We didn't get television up here in North Haversham; we weren't on the cable line. Mr. Sobel, my science teacher, taped the news for us and showed us at school.

"The boy's father died five days ago," Gran said. "He was some bigshot at the plant. Radiation killed him."

At least he hadn't died here.

Gran said, "Morning after the accident, they evacuated the boy and his mother along with the rest of them from Cookshire."

I mashed my fork into the soft, rubbery apples.

"Took them over to Mount Anthony first. The emergency people checked Mrs. Trent and the boy in, then transported them straight to the hospital. The boy, Ezra, was in shock and sick to his stomach. But he's a stubborn one. His mother said until he started with the fever and the runs, he refused to leave his father's side."

I put down my fork.

For a moment I let myself think about my own father. He left when my mother got sick. Said he loved her too much to watch her die. Dropped us here for Gran and Gramp to tend.

I can't think he cared that much about me. If he did, he would have stayed. He didn't have to watch *me* die.

My father was the first to leave me. He sure wasn't the last. I shrugged off the thought of him. I didn't like remembering him.

"How are we going to take care of the farm and the boy, too?" I asked. In my heart I knew that boy was going to die. Sure as ewes lamb in spring, he was going to die.

"Mrs. Trent and the boy have no place to go," Gran said. "No home. No money. They left everything behind in Cookshire. Everything, Nyle. There's a lot of folks scared of them. Afraid of the radiation they might be carrying."

I chased a piece of pie crust around the table with my fingertip, thinking Muncie and her parents counted among

the ones afraid.

"Mrs. Trent's not sick. She'll tend to the boy's medical needs," Gran said. "But he needs more than medicine."

"How old is he?" I asked.

"Fifteen, I think."

An oily darkness closed over me. He's fifteen, two years older than me, and he's going to die in that room.

Gran sat back in the kitchen chair and studied a cobweb stretching from one ceiling beam to another.

"Why did this have to happen?" I asked.

Gran looked at me. "You're not the only one asking that question."

"I don't make friends easy, Gran," I said. Especially not with boys.

I didn't want to go back to that room. "Can't we put them someplace else?"

Gran looked around the low-ceilinged kitchen. "Where else? In the living room? That's freezing. They need warmth, and they need a bathroom nearby."

Gran got up from the table. Her bun sagged in its net at the base of her neck. She put my uneaten cheese back in the refrigerator and dumped my demolished pie into the compost bucket beside the sink.

Gran stood at the kitchen window, looking up across the back pasture, up toward Muncie's house. She spoke so softly I had to lean forward in my chair to hear her.

"I know you'd rather not get involved in this mess, Nyle. But sometimes you *have* to do things you'd rather not."

"Well, I'm not making friends with a dead boy."

"He's not dead yet," Gran said.

"He will be if he stays in that room."

"Look," Gran said, "it's good to be with people, Nyle, even if they aren't going to be around for long. *Especially* if they're not going to be around for long. Makes being here on this earth worthwhile."

"Is that where Caleb's been all afternoon?" I asked. "Down in the back bedroom with them?"

Gran nodded. "He's got them cornered back there like a couple of stray sheep."

"Good," I said. "Let Caleb watch over them."

"Caleb's a fine dog, but he can't do everything that needs doing," Gran said.

"I know that."

A truck rattled down our driveway, its brakes squealing as it stopped outside the kitchen door.

"That'll be Red," Gran said, pulling on her coat and boots.

I shrugged into my outside clothes, grabbed my mask, and came up behind her.

Pulling her own mask up from around her neck, Gran led the way out the door.

 Three

I sat in the dark, the radio playing softly on my nightstand. Science class kept echoing in my mind. Today was our first full day back at school since the accident. Instead of his regular lesson plan, Mr. Sobel had talked about nuclear stuff.

I liked it better when science didn't come so close to home. When it fit neatly inside a textbook, with five questions at the end of each chapter, questions easily answered if you read the assigned pages.

The accident last week raised questions hard to answer, scary questions.

I couldn't get away from it. My cousin Bethany so sick. My aunt and uncle's farm ruined. And now this boy and his mother downstairs in the back bedroom.

"Sometimes you have to do things you'd rather not," Gran had said. Like listening to Ripley insult Muncie. Like digging a grave in the frozen ground for a dead sheep.

Mr. Sobel had said certain radioactive waste could kill plant and animal life for a thousand years. Radioactive particles traveled through air, through water, through earth. Government and industries had been generating deadly waste since World War II, and they still couldn't safely contain it. Now there would be so much more waste, just from the cleanup at the Cookshire plant.

I thought about the boy downstairs, Ezra. Pulling my radiation mask out of my pocket, my rough hands snagged the fine gauze.

I rubbed the material between my fingers. How could such a thin weave protect me from death? You can't see radiation, or smell it, or feel it. Could a mask stop it so easily?

Bayley padded softly up from the kitchen.

I clicked my tongue against the roof of my mouth twice, and Bayley crouched and jumped to join me on the window seat. He climbed into my lap, circled, and curled against my stomach.

How long had it been since I'd used the bathroom? Certainly not since I'd come home from school. I moved Bayley a little so he'd put less pressure on my bladder. The bathroom was downstairs, across the hall from the back bedroom.

I tried finding a comfortable position. "Maybe people will wear masks all the time," I told Bayley. "Forever. And special protective clothing. They'll have to make masks for animals." I put the gauze mask over Bayley's face. His gold eyes opened wide and the white tip of his tail twitched.

You couldn't make a cat wear a mask. You couldn't keep a mask on a sheep, either. How would a sheep graze with a mask on? *What* would a sheep graze? All the animals in the contaminated zones would either starve to death or die—from eating radioactive grass, drinking radioactive water.

It scared me, thinking about a world polluted by radiation.

What if everything died off but people? People wrapped in special space suits, eating imitation food. No more touching. Even if people wanted to touch. Even if they really wanted to. No more touching skin to skin, because of the radiation. How long could humans last that way?

I really needed to use the bathroom and it was too cold to go outside.

I made my way silently down the stairs. The kitchen closed itself in darkness. The woodstove clanked and ticked as dampered logs shifted and settled in the firebox. The kettle of water on the stove murmured to itself.

I craned my head around the stovepipe to see Gran's door. Closed, no light. The whisper of the radio came softly to my ears. She even slept with the radio on since the accident.

Stepping silently across the rippled linoleum, I headed for the bathroom.

When I came out, the back bedroom door stood open before me. It stood wide open for the first time since Gramp died.

I paused in the middle of the hallway.

Caleb kept watch, alert on the scrap-wool runner. I took a step toward the door, bent down, stroked Caleb's silky fur. He turned his head as I came forward and sniffed my leg. I dared a quick glance into the silent room.

The light from the bathroom spilled across the hall, throwing shadows on the drab green-and-gold wallpaper.

On the foldaway cot, a woman—the mother I guess, Mrs. Trent—lay on her side, blankets mounded over a slender shoulder. On the other bed, the dying bed, a boy with dark curly hair lay on his back. He stared at the ceiling.

I held still, my heart thudding in my chest. I don't know what I'd expected, but the sight of that sleepless boy rattled me.

I remembered what Gran said, about Ezra staying at his father's bedside in the hospital. His father had been a bigshot at the plant.

My fingers laced through the fur on Caleb's neck. I felt like a stranger in my own house, stooping there, staring at the boy, but I couldn't move.

Why had I come across the hall anyway? Why didn't I just use the bathroom and head straight back upstairs?

I wanted to see what he looked like. That's why. Before he died, I wanted to see him.

My legs cramped from crouching. My feet went numb. I had to get up and move.

Maybe I made a noise as I stood. I don't know.

Slowly the boy turned, staring at me with those unblinking eyes.

Caleb got up and stood beside me.

Feeling the dog against my leg brought some comfort. I had the urge to stamp the life back into my feet so I could leave. But I simply stood there, waiting for the pins and needles, held by the gaze of Ezra's eyes.

Finally I felt the tingling come. I started backing away.

Softly, softly came a voice. Ezra's voice. "I had a dog."

I waited a few moments longer, in the hallway, my heart hammering, but he said no more.

As I reached the steps that led from the kitchen to my bedroom, I heard a moan behind me and then the sound of

retching.

Back up in my room, I sat on my window seat, listening—to the news on the radio, to the boy downstairs. Finally, way past midnight, I slipped into my flannel gown, slid under the quilt, and clicked the radio off.

Bayley tunneled against my ribs and started purring.

I whispered to the quiet dark. "He had a dog."

Bayley made a little *mreep* in the back of his throat and moved closer.

I wondered if going across the hall tonight was part of doing something you'd rather not. I'd taken the first step toward that room and the boy whose fate was sealed by his presence in it.

And tomorrow, even though I'd rather not, I'd be going back to that room again.

 *Four*

Plunging my stinging hands deep inside my pockets, I pulled my arms tight to my sides and tried to hold my shivering in. The harsh November wind cut through my mask.

Muncie rocked from side to side as we waited for the bus in a small square of sunlight by the shoulder of the road. Behind us, the green iron bridge with its wood–planked roadway spanned the river.

"You look tired," Muncie said through her mask. Her voice sounded high and thin, like a child fretting.

Under the gauze I licked my chapped lips. My lips and cheeks were always too red, like I wore makeup. Gran said the high coloring came from spending so much time outdoors, but plenty people spent time outside—they didn't all look like me. "Late night," I said, turning my back against a gust.

"You never came up to do homework."

I shrugged. "No time."

A knot tightened in my stomach. It would be hard finding time for Muncie, what with chores and now Ezra and Mrs. Trent.

"Did you finish the essay for English?"

I nodded. My head itched under my wool hat.

Gran had handed me the hat earlier, as I headed out the kitchen door.

"Pull it down over your ears," she said.

My hair is fine and the color of light honey. It stands up crazy whenever I wear a hat.

"I don't need a hat."

"Wear it anyway."

I tugged the hat down hard on my head, feeling nasty.

"Seen the boy yet?" Gran asked.

"Yes," I answered.

The lines in Gran's face barely shifted as she nodded.

"Nyle?" Muncie said. "I asked what you wrote about for English."

I blinked. The cold made my eyes water. What was taking the bus so long?

"Do you think M.C. should have left the mountain?" Muncie asked.

"What mountain?"

"Sarah's mountain." Muncie's voice frosted with exasperation.

"Oh . . . M.C. Higgins." Muncie was talking about the book we'd just finished for English, about this backwoods boy and his family. "Yes. They should have left. It was a mountain of death. I'm sure it got them in the end, after the story."

Muncie looked down at her boots. "I was glad they stayed. They belonged there. They had a place for themselves there. Maybe they couldn't have fit in anyplace else."

"Maybe," I said, "but then again, maybe if they'd moved, their lives might have changed for the better."

"They were going to die," Muncie said. "Whether they moved or stayed. I'm glad they stayed."

"Do you think people from the nuclear accident should have stayed where they were?" I asked.

"Yes," Muncie said. "No."

I stared at her.

"I don't know. I just don't want them near me." Muncie kicked a stone into the road with the toe of her boot. "You coming up today after chores?"

"I can't. Gran needs me home."

"What for?"

"You want to ask her?"

Muncie usually stayed clear of Gran.

She blinked behind her glasses. "What's so important at your house?"

Looking up the valley, I shrugged. The river, sluggish with cold, idled beside the road.

I glanced beyond the front pasture dotted with sheep, my eyes lingering on the curtained window. I wanted to tell Muncie about Ezra but I didn't dare.

"I just promised my grandmother I'd stay home, that's all."

Muncie kicked another stone into the road.

"It's nothing personal, Munce."

"You don't want to study with me, do you?"

I made a face she couldn't see because of my mask.

"It's because of what Ripley said yesterday, isn't it? You think I'm stupid too." Muncie pushed her glasses up on the bridge of her nose, magnifying her eyes.

I stood with my back to the wind, shielding her from the frigid gusts. Even though her parents sent her down the hill each morning, bundled from head to toe in heavy clothing, I still felt a need to protect her. She was so small.

I pulled my hat off and scratched my head. The wind divided the strands of my hair, snapping them against my eyes.

Muncie played with the zipper on her coat.

"Muncie." I looked down at her. "Don't let what Ripley said yesterday bother you."

"It doesn't."

Resting my watery gaze on the dull green carpet of the hillside, I felt the crush of all I stood to lose because of the accident. It broke over my head like a slough of snow.

"I just want to make sure it's not bothering *you*," Muncie said through her mask.

"It's not."

Color flushed above the mask line, around the edges of Muncie's cheeks.

"Then what *is* bothering you?" she asked.

"Nothing."

"Is it something to do with me?"

"Why does everything have to be about you?" I asked.

"It doesn't," Muncie said. "Is that the way I act?"

I nodded. The cold made the inside of my nose crinkle.

"You don't really like me, do you," Muncie said. "You just put up with me because I live on your grandmother's land."

I scowled at Muncie. "Of course I like you. You're my best friend. Quit acting like a baby. You're always acting like a baby."

"I am not," Muncie said. "How am I acting like a baby?"

"Well—about our being friends. Why do you even have to ask? It's stupid. And the way you are about boys."

Muncie reached up and punched me with her pudgy fist. "What do boys have to do with it?"

"Nothing."

"You don't like anybody, do you?"

I pinched the end of my nose through my mask. My fingers stung. I wished Gran had handed me a pair of gloves when she gave me the hat.

Peering up the road, I watched for the bus. Its engine growled as it slowed at the Hulls'. The Hulls were one of a handful of families along our road who hadn't bolted after the accident.

Muncie dropped her head to one side. "Do you like somebody, Nyle?" she asked.

I thought about Ezra, staring at the ceiling last night. I thought about his curly hair in the darkness. I thought about him being in the back bedroom, in the dying room.

"No," I said. "I don't."

 *Five*

I got through school that day, and evening chores, too. Heading straight up to my room, I turned on the radio. The newsman went on and on, reporting the problems faced by emergency units at the nuclear plant.

As I listened, I slowly inspected my room, touching all the treasures on my shelves, treasures I would lose if we evacuated. I had river rocks, acorns, birds' nests and feathers, amber glass, a tarnished belt buckle, a box of old watch faces: all kinds of stuff crowded on my shelves. If the wind turned this way, radiation would contaminate every bit of it.

On the shelf of my nightstand I kept the handful of books I'd chosen in R.I.F. distributions over the years. I read the titles on the slim spines.

The back bedroom and Ezra made me real uneasy, but somehow I'd have to go down there. I couldn't see myself talking much to that boy, but I guessed I could read to him.

Swaggering across the floor, Bayley climbed my jeans leg with his front claws.

"You want to come see Ezra?" I asked, lifting the cat up and rubbing the short hair under his chin with my index finger.

Bayley purred and stretched his neck out, giving my fingers a longer path to travel.

"Bayley, you lucky old cat, you don't ever have to do anything you'd rather not."

I could read to Ezra from *M.C. Higgins, the Great*, but I'd just finished reading that for school. I really didn't care to read it again so soon. Plus there were some embarrassing parts for a girl to read to a boy.

My hand stopped on *Slake's Limbo*, my choice at the R.I.F. distribution two years ago, when I was in sixth grade. I never had much time for reading, but I sure read that book. At least four times. Slake was all alone in his world. I knew how he felt, just how he felt. But it was so much worse for him, never going outside the train station. Never seeing daylight. What would it be like, never seeing the light of day?

I pulled the book off my shelf and thought about the boy downstairs, about the drawn curtain in the back bedroom. This was the right book. There couldn't be a more right book.

Coming down the steps, I ran my fingers through my hair, trying to make myself presentable. The kitchen smelled of yeast. Bread rising. When Gran came in from chopping wood, the aroma of baking loaves would fill the house.

I cleared my throat, tugged at my sweatshirt, and slouched down the hall.

As I came to the back bedroom, a woman rose from the worn, flowered chair beside the boy's bed. From the hallway she looked young, her slim face framed by shoulder-length hair.

"You must be Nyle," the woman said. She had an accent. Very formal, very elegant. "I am Mrs. Trent."

She put her hand out, saw my rough, dirty nails, and hesitated a moment. The skin on the back of her hand gave her age away, late forties, early fifties. We shook hands.

"Please," Mrs. Trent said, "come with me into the hall." She looked down once on Ezra, then led the way slowly out of the room, closing the back bedroom door behind her.

I didn't like her shutting the door on the boy like that, shutting him inside, alone, in the dying room.

"Thank you for inviting us into your home," Mrs. Trent said. She moved stiffly. Tiny wrinkles clustered around the outsides of her large eyes, green eyes, the color of new acorns. The clothes she wore didn't suit her, a threadbare housedress, an old sweater, brown sandals.

The evacuees brought nothing of their own out of the contamination zone. The taint of radiation spoiled everything, even their shoes. They all wore donated clothing.

Mrs. Trent's hair was only a little shorter than mine, and styled the same way, parted on the side and swingy. Hers was wavy, though, while mine hung straight.

"You have brought a book," Mrs. Trent said. "Could I see it?"

I turned the book cover side up, so she could read the title.

"I have never heard of this," Mrs. Trent said.

"It's about a boy who lives in a train station. I thought I could read a little to Ezra. I mean if that's all right."

"He may not hear you," she said. "The doctors told us we might have a few more days before he got sick again. The illness returned much sooner than they thought."

I nodded.

"I hope you do not mind too much our being here."

I looked down at my feet. There was a hole in the toe of my right sock.

"I worry that your friends might disapprove of our staying in your home."

I thought about Muncie and shrugged.

"Perhaps you do not wish to discuss such things. Ezra, too, keeps certain thoughts to himself. At the hospital Ezra hid his sickness so he might remain near his father."

Something caught in her throat. Her green eyes turned away from me. "Then he could not hide his sickness any longer. The doctors did what they could for him. We came here. He has not spoken a word since."

I felt a pressure in my throat like a thumb against my windpipe.

"His fever is rising." Mrs. Trent swallowed, lifting her chin as she did. "I hope you do not mind sitting with him. He must not be alone."

She stepped aside and opened the back bedroom door again.

Ezra hadn't moved. He lay on his back, his head pressed deep into the feather pillow.

His eyes had an unusual shape, something I hadn't seen in

the dark last night. They drooped down at the sides. It made his face different from any I had seen before. Above one eyebrow was a small crescent-shaped scar.

There was a smell of illness in the room, the old smell that had been there when Gramp died, when my mother died. Ezra's large hands lay on top of the quilt. He wore what looked like Gramp's old pajamas.

Caleb dozed beside the door.

I knelt down and stroked the dog's side.

Lifting his head, Caleb dragged a wet tongue over my hand, then flopped back down, sighed, and went to sleep again.

Mrs. Trent's eyes rested a moment on Ezra before she left the room.

A night-light glowed in the wall outlet. The light from the hallway crept across the oval rug. The curtain remained tightly shut.

"Hi," I said. "Ezra?"

Ezra didn't move, except for the labored rise and fall of his chest as he struggled to breathe.

I should just leave him to die in peace.

But Gran wanted me to stay. Mrs. Trent wanted me to stay.

I didn't know what else to do, so I opened the book and started reading aloud by the light from the hallway.

After a few moments Ezra turned his head toward me and opened his eyes.

He blinked, stared, trying, I think, to bring me into focus.

"I'm Nyle Sumner," I said. "You're in my house."

Ezra nodded. It looked as if it hurt him to move. He shut his eyes again.

I sat anxiously in the flowered chair, trying not to breathe too deeply. I still worried about catching the radiation from him, even though Gran said I couldn't.

"Do you know this book?" I asked.

Ezra kept his eyes closed. His breathing sounded like the crunch of feet over gravel. He moved his legs fitfully under the blanket. Every now and then a noise escaped from him, a small whimper.

"It's a good book," I said. I waited a moment. "Should I read some more to you? Should I start over?"

I started again, keeping my voice low, afraid to make too much noise on the edge of Ezra's illness.

Every now and then his eyes came open. He stared at a spot to the left of my foot, where Caleb had crept inside the room.

But he didn't look at me again.

Finally I heard Gran clanging around in the kitchen. I smelled the warm, full aroma of bread baking. Mrs. Trent came softly down the hall and motioned with her straight back and her manicured hand for me to leave.

"Thank you," she said, dismissing me.

She walked straight into the room, straight past me, over to Ezra, smoothing his curls back from his eyes. She touched her lips to his forehead.

I watched from the doorway as Mrs. Trent wrung out a washcloth and placed it over Ezra's brow. She whispered what sounded like a prayer in a language I didn't know. Ezra and his mother huddled together, alone in the dark country of his illness.

 \ *Six*

The following day it poured. Everyone feared the rain, terrified of the fallout it carried with it from the nuclear plant. Rain had turned the land between Vermont and the Atlantic Ocean into a dead zone.

Mr. Perry, our principal, used a radiation detector, better than the one Gran had at home. He measured atmospheric radiation before he sent the school buses out for us each morning. He measured it again before he let us leave each afternoon.

Shortly before lunch, ten days after the accident, Mr. Perry came on the public address system.

"They capped the nuclear leak early this morning," he said, relief rumbling his voice. "The air is safe now. The rain is safe now. We can throw away our masks."

The dozen or so kids left in my class cheered. Some went straight to the trash and tossed their masks out. I didn't. I took mine off, but I wouldn't throw it away.

Muncie didn't throw her mask out either. She had strict orders to wear it until her *parents* said she could remove it. Only Muncie's face remained covered when we boarded the bus for home. Something else making her different. Well, maybe the Harrises would let Muncie ditch the mask after today.

I stared out the bus window at abandoned houses along the road. With the plant capped, people would come back. I wanted to feel soothed, to believe everything would be all right, even with Ezra. But after the things Mr. Sobel had said about radiation and waste, I couldn't really relax.

At our stop, Muncie jumped off the bus behind me, laughing, rolling her big head on her shoulders. She let the rain beat down on her glasses, soak through her mask.

The door scissored shut behind us and the school bus pulled away.

"All safe, all safe," Muncie sang.

Walking home through the steady downpour, my hair dripped, the icy trickle ran over my cheeks and down my neck. Drops of sleety rainwater skated along Muncie's nose.

Clumsy in her bulky boots, she broad-jumped into a puddle and landed on a rock. It rolled out from under her, making her fall. Her breath sucked in with the shock of cold as she hit the water.

"You okay?" I bent over her.

Muncie made two fists and beat at the puddle, spraying a shower of frigid water over the two of us and laughing.

I shook my head. "Come on," I said, helping her to her feet.

We continued up the hill past the close-packed sheep.

The rain would be noodling its way down through the sheep's thick wool. My socks squished inside my old boots.

When we reached my drive, we stopped while Muncie caught her breath.

"How about—my house—hot chocolate?" Muncie said.

I hesitated. "Can't."

Muncie pushed her glasses back up on the bridge of her nose. "Oh," she said. Looking dejected, she started up the hill.

"You want me to wait till you get to the top?" I called to Muncie's back.

Muncie, looking like a yellow toadstool in her raincoat and hat, shrugged. "You can't," she said.

I ran up the hill to catch her. But Muncie ignored me. She just kept climbing.

The Trents had come between us that quickly. I kicked with my heavy boot at a rock stuck in the road.

But I couldn't tell her about Ezra and his mother. Maybe if Muncie didn't already have so many problems. Maybe if radiation didn't frighten her parents so much. But it did.

Instead of going straight home, I stayed out and started evening chores. Might as well. I couldn't get any wetter.

When I finally came in, Gran met me at the kitchen door with an old towel. I wrapped the towel around my shoulders and headed straight for the woodstove.

Opening my backpack, I pulled the rumpled mask out and held it dangling in the air between us. "You heard about the plant?"

Gran nodded. "Throw the mask away," she said. "I tossed mine out as soon as I heard."

But I took the mask, instead, and hung it on a hook in the kitchen. "A remembrance," I said. I hated throwing anything out.

"I've got hot chocolate for you. Dry off."

I scrubbed my hair with the towel while Gran held out a mug of cocoa. Standing in front of the stove, I turned front to back, back to front. Steam curled off my jeans.

"Ezra and Mrs. Trent still here?" I asked, swallowing the warm, sweet liquid.

"Course they are," Gran said. "Where do you think they'd be?"

I finished the cocoa, wiping the chocolate mustache from my upper lip with my thumb.

Climbing the steps to my bedroom, I peeled off my damp things and pulled on dry clothes. Over at the window I looked out across the farm, so soft in the gray wool of November. I stood there a long time before picking up Ezra's book.

Well, here goes.

But I didn't move toward the steps. I sat down instead on my bed and stroked Bayley.

My mother had died.

Gramp had died.

I lowered my cheek against Bayley's soft side. He purred, massaging my ear with sound.

Ezra would die too.

Mrs. Trent met me outside the back bedroom.

"He is worse," she said. "He has not taken any food in over a day. On the nightstand is a cloth and a bowl of sweetened water. Could you touch some to his lips while you are with him?"

I balked. Gran had promised I wouldn't be concerned with Ezra's physical needs. No bedpan. No cleaning up after Ezra when he vomited or had diarrhea. That was the deal. So what right did Mrs. Trent have, asking me to touch Ezra? My insides crawled at the thought of touching him.

But Mrs. Trent looked so exhausted.

I nodded grudgingly, not wanting to tend Ezra, but realizing tending him was one of those things I had to do even if I'd rather not. "I'll see to it. Why don't you rest awhile, Mrs. Trent?"

If she continued like this, the room would claim both of them.

But she didn't climb into her cot. She headed for the bathroom instead.

I put my book down on the flowered chair. Ezra looked smaller than he had the day before, more shrunken—emphasizing the droop of his eyes and the tiny moon-shaped scar over his brow. Every now and then a shudder ran through him, shaking his body under the blankets.

I stood for a while, reluctant to go near. At last I approached his bed. Picking up the washcloth, I dipped it into the bowl of cool water.

I touched the cloth to Ezra's lips, careful that my fingers did not brush his skin. He made a sound, a kind of groan, deep down in his throat, but he didn't open his eyes.

"It's me. Nyle Sumner. I came yesterday." I touched the cloth to Ezra's lips again.

"I've come to read some more. Would you like to hear?"

No response.

I remembered Gramp in this room. He gave up eating near the end. He liked sucking on chips of ice, though. His mouth was dry, he said. I'd wrap ice cubes in a towel and beat on them with a hammer till they slivered. Gramp would lay in bed, propped up, quietly sucking. He stared out the window while I talked about everything I could think of to hold him here. To hold him to life. Every evening before I left him, I'd tell him to wait for me, I'd be back in the morning.

He died anyway.

Gran didn't even cry. She got up the very next day and moved every length of sheep fence on our property.

And finally, after the funeral, after everybody went home and left us, I pulled my boots on and went out, and I moved fences too.

I gave Ezra a little more water, wiping my wet hands on my jeans.

Rain tapped with a steady rhythm on the metal roof above our heads. Clean rain. Radiation-free rain.

Pong. Pong. Pong. I wanted to listen. I wanted to watch it. I hoped it would turn to snow. I started slowly toward the window. We didn't need to keep the curtain closed anymore; we didn't need to protect Ezra from radiation. He was safe, all of us outside the contamination zone were safe. I reached out to yank the curtain open and let in the good dark, the clean dark.

Mrs. Trent appeared at my side. "Do not touch that, please," she said.

I jumped.

"He wishes this," Mrs. Trent said. "That the curtain remain closed."

Lowering myself into the flowered chair, I gripped the thin book in my fist and waited for her to leave.

 \ *Seven*

When Muncie asked why I never came to visit, I ignored her rather than tell a lie. I couldn't tell her the truth. People didn't need much of a reason for leaving. How could I trust the Harrises to stay when they had so many good reasons to go?

When we entered history class one day, Mrs. Haskins was back. She looked up from an article she was reading and nodded at us.

After the accident at the power plant, Mrs. Haskins had taken a leave of absence. A lot of teachers had. So far, only a few had come back.

She was a good teacher, Mrs. Haskins. She made history interesting.

The bell rang for class to start and Mrs. Haskins stood up, holding the newspaper she'd been reading.

Walking around to the front of her desk, she half-sat, half-leaned on the wooden edge.

Mrs. Haskins came from Boston originally. She talked with a Boston accent. In her mind, the *Globe* was the final word on everything. But the paper she held today wasn't the *Globe*. She couldn't possibly read to us from the *Globe* today, because the *Boston Globe* had ceased to exist. Boston had ceased to exist. The buildings still stood, the houses, the traffic lights, the shops, the parks. The offices of the *Boston Globe* still existed. But no people remained, no people at all.

What if some of her family or friends hadn't made it out all right?

"We're going to let Chester Arthur rest a little longer," Mrs. Haskins said. "I want to talk about something else today."

I ran my finger back and forth across the sharp corner of my history book.

"Just capping the leak doesn't end this emergency, you know," Mrs. Haskins began.

A familiar knot tightened in my stomach.

Mrs. Haskins said, "You've been talking about nuclear issues in your science class."

Dan Taylor leaned forward, took off his hat, set it on his desk. Dan always wore that fedora hat, his father's suit jacket, and blue jeans. It surprised me Dan's family had stayed through the accident. They seemed the kind to leave.

Mrs. Haskins took a deep breath and let it back out again. "Millions of people are homeless, jobless, separated from loved ones. Hundreds died trying to get away, thousands will die later, from cancer."

Ripley said, "Boston was too crowded anyway."

A few kids snickered.

"Using radioactive fallout as a form of population control is a pretty frightening concept," Mrs. Haskins said.

Ripley Powers glared at Mrs. Haskins with his good eye.

I raised my hand, my finger pressed over a bloody spot where I'd picked a hangnail. "Will we be part of the thousands with cancer?"

I tried to keep breathing. Both my mother and Gramp had died of cancer.

The kids in the class looked at Mrs. Haskins.

"I don't know," she said. "It really is only a matter of which way the wind blew, where the rain fell. The accident *will* touch each of us in some way."

Was she thinking about her family from Boston?

"Those of you whose folks farm, or garden, or raise livestock—how safe will it be to use your land over the next years? No one knows."

My stomach twisted, thinking about it all. Our sheep, and our woodlot, Aunt May and Uncle Lemmy, Bethany, and Ezra.

"What I want you to do today," Mrs. Haskins said, "is write to our congressmen. Write to our senators. Tell them what it's like here now. Right now. Tell them everything. And ask them what they plan to do about it."

We sat silently at our desks, while Mrs. Haskins put the names of the politicians on the blackboard. None of us seemed to know what to write.

At the end of the period, we filed slowly out of her room, leaving Mrs. Haskins at her desk, staring out the window.

That evening, in the back bedroom, I didn't even try to read. I just sat, holding the book, gazing at Ezra, willing him to live. My eyes traced over and over the small scar above his eyebrow.

He hadn't moved in days.

A visiting nurse had come twice. He had Ezra hooked up to an I.V. suspended from a wooden coatrack.

Mrs. Trent showed signs of radiation sickness now too, though not nearly as bad as Ezra. The nurse taught Gran to take care of them both, to change sheets without moving them out of bed, to keep them hydrated. The nurse said Gran was doing everything that could be done. Small comfort.

As sick as Mrs. Trent was, she got a little easier to be with. She listened when I read to Ezra, even if he wasn't listening.

One night Mrs. Trent talked, her accented voice barely above a whisper.

"I wish my parents had met Ezra," she said as I adjusted her pillow. "Before all of this."

I looked down at her, unsure of what to say.

"They are Israeli," she said. "My parents. They risked their lives to be Israeli. Perhaps I should have brought him to them. They would have been so proud."

"Maybe you still can bring him," I said.

Our eyes traveled over Ezra's laboring body, then returned to each other. I looked away first.

"They did not understand how I could marry out of my faith," Mrs. Trent said.

I sat on the side of her cot.

"My parents survived the Holocaust. You know the Holocaust?"

I nodded.

"I did not mean to break their hearts," Mrs. Trent said. "But I fell in love with Ezra's father. Now I am paying."

I almost took her in my arms to comfort her. Almost.

Ezra wandered somewhere deep in his illness. His large hands balled up in fists outside the blankets. His curly hair matted where it met the pillow.

While Mrs. Trent slept, I studied the straight line of Ezra's nose. His lips cracked from loss of fluids. I tried to remember the color of his open eyes.

One night after sitting in silence for an hour, clasping *Slake's Limbo* to my chest, I stood to leave.

"I've got a lot of homework to do," I said.

Ezra's lips moved. He said something.

The next moment, though, he looked as empty as before.

But I'd heard him. He'd spoken.

"What did you say?" I asked. "What is it, Ezra?"

But he was gone again.

I turned to Mrs. Trent, staring at me, her green eyes wide with fear. She'd heard Ezra too. I could tell by her expression. She breathed in and out so rapidly.

Mrs. Trent motioned me over. She reached out and took my hand.

"Can I get you something?" I asked.

"Sit, please," she said.

I wiped her forehead with a wet cloth. Her cheeks burned red and her eyes glistened. She shut her lids and shuddered.

"His father spoke too," she said, gripping my arm. "Once. And then he died."

 *Eight*

From one day to the next Ezra never stirred. Not once. He remained still, silent, unchanging. But he didn't die.

I read to him, wet his lips with a cloth. I don't think Ezra knew I was there. I don't think he knew anything.

The rain continued to fall. Mr. Sobel, the science teacher, monitored it. Mrs. Haskins monitored it. Gran monitored it. She found traces of radioactivity sometimes, but always it was within a normal range.

Nearly bare trees brushed against a low, dark sky. Brittle leaves clung, quaking in the wind.

I sat with Ezra and Mrs. Trent. Even though Ezra showed no sign of hearing me, I told him about my classes. Softly I sang him the songs from chorus. I'd done all these things with Gramp, too, trying to keep him from leaving.

Once, I thought Ezra's hand moved as I sang "Tender Shepherd"—a song from our Christmas concert. I stared at his fingers, concentrating all my will into making them move again. They didn't.

I told Ezra every dumb joke I could remember hearing at school. Really dumb jokes. I never told jokes. I wasn't any good at it. Besides, I didn't think these jokes were very funny. Mrs. Trent didn't think they were funny either. If she understood them, she never laughed. But I told jokes just the same. And when I ran out of jokes I just sat there, looking around the room, remembering.

Gran's dusty cookie tins sat stacked in the corner beside the dresser, against the green-and-gold striped wallpaper. Gran used to bake like crazy—not just bread. I remember loving this room then. I'd sleep in it sometimes. There was a great big crib, just for me, right under the window. I could see it in my mind. It always felt warm and welcoming in this room.

At Christmastime those tins would fill with cookies, crisp sugar cookies with sprinkles on top, powdery cookies that left a sweet white dust on my fingertips, and my favorite ones—the round butter cookies with the chocolate kiss in the top. My father and I would sneak back here and raid the cookie tins while Mama and Gran and Gramp visited. When my mother would come down the hall, she'd catch us with our mouths full. She'd scold my father, then eat a cookie herself. I don't know why I remembered that, sitting with Ezra. It happened so long ago. Back before my father left, before my mother left. People always leaving.

How could Gran make me stay in this room and watch it again?

Late that night, as I sat upstairs in my window seat, the wind finally herded the clouds off. Stars appeared, brilliant, sharp-edged, scattered like hard white seeds across the black sky.

Morning came on as clear and blue as ice melt. At the bus stop Muncie swayed around me like an eager puppy.

"It's going to be nice all day," she said. "Let's gather wool this afternoon. My basket is nearly full."

All summer and early fall, Muncie and I had gathered bits and pieces of pulled wool. Muncie kept the wool in a basket at her house.

"I don't know, Munce. I promised Gran I'd move the flock of yearlings in the front pasture today."

"I'll help," Muncie offered.

After school I left my backpack in the shed, pulled on my work boots, and let Caleb out.

Coming past the end of the house, I avoided looking at the drawn curtain. I ran to meet Muncie on the dirt road.

Disconnecting the clip feeding power to the fence, I motioned Muncie to join me. Caleb whined at my side, eager to work.

Muncie clumped along on her short legs as she helped me set the fence for the new pasture. She'd watched me set fences a hundred times; she knew how to extend the metal webbing, was good at it. Though half my size, Muncie had double my strength.

As soon as we'd defined the borders of the pasture with the fencing, I let Muncie inside with the sheep. She tried playing follow-the-leader with the closest ewe, her hands reaching for the rump of raw wool, but the sheep kept out of her reach.

They were like big toys to Muncie. I tended them. She played with them. That's how it was with Muncie. I couldn't count on her for the serious stuff. But that was okay. I could count on her to be there.

The lambs skittered across the pasture away from her.

Down the hill, Ripley Powers strode along the main road in his camouflage suit, a rifle cradled in his arms like a rigid snake. Tyrus ran ahead.

Ripley kept yelling for Tyrus to heel. His voice carried through the thin air, all the way up where I stood in the pasture.

Deer season. That would keep Ripley and Tyrus out of our hair for a few weeks.

"Ready to move these sheep?" I asked Muncie.

Caleb sat, panting slightly, head cocked to one side, ears alert, waiting for the command. I whistled.

"Get out away, Caleb. Good boy."

Caleb streaked toward the large flock of yearlings. As he got close, he slowed, crouching low. His dark eyes flashed and the sheep moved uneasily away from him.

Two sheep broke from the flock. Caleb shot after them.

"Come by, Caleb," I called. "Come by, boy."

Caleb slunk along, directing the sheep with his eyes, pressing them through the opening in the fence.

He herded the flock into the far corner of the new pasture. "That'll do," I said, closing them in.

Caleb relaxed and pranced around my legs. I dismantled the fencing from the old pasture and rolled it up. Muncie helped.

"Let's check the barbed fences for wool," she said when we'd finished.

I scooped some fresh salt out of the big container and

poured it inside the feeder in the new pasture, checking once more that all was well.

"Okay," I said. "You want to gather wool? We'll gather wool. Let's go."

We climbed up and down the rolling hills of Gran's land, Muncie's head bobbing along at my elbow. Combing the fences, moving from pasture to pasture, we searched for pulled wool. Every time she discovered some, Muncie'd yell. She'd lift her hand to show me her find before shoving the bit of wool into her basket.

By the time we headed for home, our stomachs were rumbling. Lights winked and sparkled across the valley. Up at the farmhouse, I could see Gran moving in the kitchen.

Through the woods, a light from Ripley's trailer shifted between branches. And up at the top of the hill, set back in the trees, a glimpse of twinkling from Muncie's house.

Muncie had finally gathered enough wool to fill her basket. I mashed the itchy white snags down so she wouldn't lose any on the way home. "You wash this tonight and let it dry. I'll come this weekend and help you card and spin it."

Before heading in, I fed the sheep in the barn and reconnected the electric fence. Hoisting my backpack up onto my shoulder, I passed the closed curtain of Ezra's room. I felt an unexpected tug.

Dragging an armload of wood over to the house, I stomped the dirt off my boots before coming into the kitchen. Gran stood at the sink, washing dishes. Half a loaf of fresh bread sat on the table.

"You're out late. Sheep give you any trouble?" Gran asked.

"No," I answered. "I just felt like staying out." I dropped the dry wood into the keeping box.

"You know Mrs. Trent won't leave that room unless you're down there with Ezra," Gran said. "She's been waiting her supper till you came."

I shoved my raw hands into my jean pockets.

"Come eat," Gran said. "You must be starved. You can take your homework and do it in Ezra's room right after."

"I can't do my homework in there." I could hardly think straight in that room. "Gran—he doesn't even know I'm there. I could skip one night."

"No you can't."

"Why are you making me do this?" I asked. "I don't want to do this."

Gran leaned back against the sink. "You're doing it because it's right, Nyle. Times like this we've got to do what's right. Look out for each other. Take care of each other. You understand?"

I shrugged.

"Eat your soup, Nyle."

What else could I do? I dipped my spoon inside the soup bowl, and I ate.

Ezra hadn't moved or spoken for almost a week. For almost a week the person inside Ezra's body wandered further and further from life.

I wished he'd just make up his mind to die and get it over with.

Standing beside the flowered chair, I felt a black and bitter anger. At Gran, at Mrs. Trent, at this room. A few stubborn tears pushed their way to my eyes. Mrs. Trent had left the room as soon as I had come, hobbling out, pitiful, a shadow of the elegant woman who had come to us weeks before.

Suddenly a voice creaked below me in the darkness. "You crying?"

"What?"

I turned toward Ezra, but my eyes, filmy with tears, couldn't see him. Hands shaking, I switched on the dresser lamp.

Ezra groaned, reacting to the light. How long had it been since he'd reacted to light?

Switching the lamp back off, I quickly brushed the tears from my cheeks with the backs of my hands.

A long sigh from the bed.

"Ezra?"

"Hmmm?" More of a croak than a voice.

He was awake!

Ezra sighed and shut his eyes. Those drooping eyes.

Don't leave again, I thought in a panic.

"Ezra!" Words tumbled out of me. "Wait. Don't go."

Ezra's eyes stayed closed. "Nowhere to go," he whispered. The last word trailed off.

"Ezra?" I came close, standing directly over the bed. "I know you need to rest. And I have a lot of homework waiting for me. But I'll be back tomorrow."

Ezra's face looked the same as it had over the last few weeks. Empty.

"Ezra, will you wait till tomorrow?"

His tongue came out, ran lightly over his lips. "You bet, Shep."

 \ *Nine*

Muncie and I sat on her living-room rug, in front of a crackling fire. The storm outside darkened the room; Mrs. Harris put on lights. If I were a cat, I would have purred, it was so snug in that house.

I had brought along two sets of carding paddles from the shed. Muncie and I sat with a fistful of wool in each of our laps. We brushed the short hanks so all the strands of wool ran in one direction.

In the spring, before lambing, Gran and I spent days shearing all our sheep. We never carded or spun the wool ourselves. We sent our bags of raw wool to The Spinnery in Putney. I wondered what we'd do this spring, now that The Spinnery had closed.

When she was young, Gran used to wash and comb and spin the wool herself. But hardly anyone did it by hand anymore. Maybe that was another thing that would change because of the accident.

A log settled in the fireplace, sending sparks flying. I stopped carding long enough to flick a live coal back into the flames.

Gran had a fireplace in her bedroom and there was another in the dining room, but we never used either of them. Only the woodstove in the kitchen.

"It's nice having a fire with the snow coming down," I said.

Muncie's face shifted into a grin under her mask, making her glasses raise up. 'Yeah, thanks, Daddy."

"You're welcome." Mr. Harris sat in the big gold chair under the window, reading the Burlington paper. He had two other newspapers stacked up beside him. Job hunting. He'd run a car dealership in Cookshire before the accident. All those cars still sat on the lot, shiny, only a couple of miles on their odometers. No one would ever own those cars. No one would ever drive them. They'd rust, the tires crack and give out, they'd turn to dust where they sat.

"How fast is your batch coming?" Muncie asked, leaning around me to see how much wool I'd carded so far. "I bet I can comb more than you can."

"I don't want to race, Muncie," I said.

Carding wool reminded me of brushing doll's hair. I didn't like that, either.

I had a doll once. She came dressed in pale blue overalls with elastic around her ankles and tiny pink flowers on her shirt. She was a gift from my mother, given to me when we moved in with Gran and Gramp.

The doll's fine hair matched my own, and my mother's, too. I guess that's why she chose her. The whole time of my mother's illness, I kept the doll perfect.

I was six when my mother died. I hardly remember anything before that. There aren't pictures. But I do remember that doll.

Mostly Gran and Gramp kept me out of the back bedroom during my mother's illness. Then one day they let me in.

I was so eager to see her. I burst in, raced over to the bed. I touched her hand. Cold. I'd expected to find my mother sitting up, deep-voiced and smiling. Her withered body barely rippled the sheets. I stepped back, terrified. That was not my mother. That could not be my mother.

Her foul breath rattled in her throat like wind worrying a sheet on the line.

Something changed in the room. I felt it inside my chest. The air weighed too much, and then it weighed nothing at all.

Gran said, "She's gone."

Someone, a neighbor I think, pulled the sheet up, covering her face, her patchy bald head.

Someone else reached for my hand.

I broke away and ran up the stairs. I hid in the knee-wall under the eaves, taking my doll with me.

Huddled among the cobwebs and the mouse droppings, I cowered, trembling for hours.

Gramp found me. He pulled me out, and after calming me, he plunked me into the bathtub. I came clean, more or less, but my doll didn't. Filth caked her clothing, her hair tangled hopelessly.

Days later, while Gran and Gramp attended my mother's funeral, Aunt May stayed with me, sitting silently in the kitchen.

I spent the whole morning shivering in my room, though the house wasn't cold. I just kept shaking inside. I dragged my brush through the doll's hair, over and over, working away at the snarls until the last hair lay smooth.

But I'd pulled so much hair out in the process, the doll was nearly bald. Her rubber scalp showed dull orange. The dark holes of hair shafts curved around the scalp in a pattern. The doll's baldness terrified me. I wrapped it in a pillowcase and buried it in the trash.

"It's really coming down," Muncie said. "How many inches do you think we have already?"

I looked out the window.

"How many you think, Nyle?"

I watched the snow fall outside Muncie's living-room window, large, grayish flakes drifting softly past the glass. "I don't know."

We carded wool until lunchtime. Muncie eyed the short, neat hanks proudly. "Look how much we did."

"Mostly how much you did," I said. "You're good at this, Muncie."

Muncie acted silly, clumping around to hide her pleasure.

"Let's start spinning right after lunch," she said.

"I can't. I need to get home early this afternoon. There's always extra chores after a snow."

Muncie pulled me into her bedroom, a room not much bigger than a closet. I sat on the edge of her spread. Shelves ran along each wall beneath the windows. And on all of those shelves were books, hundreds of books. Like a real library.

"Is your grandmother sick?" Muncie asked. "Is that why

you're spending so much time in your house? Is that why you keep that curtain closed?"

I turned away so she couldn't see my face. "Gran, sick?" I shook my head.

"Then tell me. If your grandmother's not sick, what's going on at your house that you don't have time for me anymore?"

I thought about Ezra struggling back. I didn't dare say anything to jinx him. The Harrises were getting along all right. They weren't in such a hurry to leave anymore. But if I told them about Ezra, that might change everything.

"It's just something I can't talk about."

Muncie looked crushed. I wanted to tell her. I wanted to talk about Ezra so much, my throat ached. But if I told, Mr. and Mrs. Harris wouldn't let me near Muncie. And they might tell everyone else about the Trents too. They weren't the only ones afraid of evacuees. And these evacuees in particular, the widow and son of the man who ran the power plant. I didn't want anyone to know.

I looked out the window at the snow. "Do you ever think about the people from the Cookshire accident," I asked, "the people who are homeless now, and sick with radiation?"

"Mutants," Muncie said, an ugly edge to her voice.

I spun around to face her.

"Muncie!"

Muncie sounded angry. "They're dangerous. My parents said so. Just being near one could kill you. They have so much radiation in their bodies, they glow."

"No they don't!" I said.

Muncie rocked over to the opposite corner of her room.

"Yes they do. I hope I never see one."

"They're not dangerous," I said. "They're sick, and alone. They need help."

"Ripley says if I ever met one of those mutants from the accident, I'd mutate too. I'd get shorter and uglier than I already am."

"Stop it," I said. "You don't believe what he says. I know you don't. You're no mutant and neither are the people from the accident."

"Since when are you an authority?" Muncie asked.

Maybe I'd said too much. "I'm not an authority."

But Muncie suddenly looked as if she knew the truth. Or at least suspected it.

I stayed until a little after two, starting Muncie on the spinning. But the snug feeling had gone. And no amount of crackling fires could bring it back.

 \ *Ten*

The deep snow hushed the house, especially Ezra's room, with the curtain drawn. But Ezra hadn't been hushed.

"Shep?" he asked as I appeared at the back-bedroom door.

He followed me with his eyes as I switched on the dresser lamp.

He was sitting up, waiting for me, two pillows propped behind his back.

"How you feeling?" I asked.

Ezra spoke in a husky whisper. "My mother said it snowed."

"I could open the curtain and show you."

"No!"

"Okay." I ran my fingers through my hair, brushing back the sides.

All those days I'd waited for Ezra to open his eyes. To

talk to me. Now we could talk, and I didn't know what to say.

"It's good you're awake," I tried again, turning back to him. "You've been pretty sick."

"Sorry." Ezra tried shrugging, but his shoulders only twitched. He licked his lips.

"Would you like something to drink? Your mother left this pink ice for you."

I eased a frozen juice chip into his mouth with a blue plastic spoon, one Gran had kept since my baby days.

"Thanks," he croaked.

"More?"

Ezra moved his head no.

"Where's the dog?"

"Caleb?" I asked. "Out with Gran."

"He's a watchdog?"

"No," I said. "A herding dog. He moves the sheep for us."

Ezra looked confused.

"We give him commands," I said. "And he does the work."

"He takes orders—from *you*?"

"Sure. Why shouldn't he?"

Ezra smiled. His eyes teased.

"Do you want me to read to you?" I asked.

Ezra nodded.

"What do you want to hear?"

"Your voice," said Ezra.

I felt heat rise into my cheeks.

"Your voice," Ezra said. "Kept finding me. When I was sick. I like your voice."

I opened *Slake's Limbo*, started reading.

Ezra watched me for a while, then shut his eyes.

I stopped and looked over at him. He was too still.

"Ezra?"

He opened his eyes, dark blue eyes. "Hmmm?"

He's all right, I told myself. Just tired. "You like the book?"

"Um-hmmm," Ezra said.

I started reading again. Finished a chapter. Closed the book on my finger.

"I think you're going to live, Ezra Trent."

Ezra sighed. "All things considered," he said, "you might be right."

I fed him another spoonful of frozen juice.

He stared up at me. "Thanks for the grub, ma'am."

It took such an effort for him to talk. I looked down at the blue plastic spoon in my hand. "It's nothing."

"No," he said wearily. "It's something. Believe me, it's something."

My hands shook. I put the spoon down.

"Hey." Ezra drew in a long breath. "You teach me about sheep?"

"You want to know about sheep?" I asked.

"Yeah." His words slurred, his eyelids drooped. "And lambs."

"No lambs until spring," I said. "Will you be here in the spring?"

He turned his eyes away, looking at his hands on the quilt. He no longer looked at me. He could be dead by spring. We both knew it.

Picking the book back up, I clasped it to my chest.

"Hey, Ezra," I said. "You'll get your first sheep-farming lesson tomorrow."

Ezra stared at the curtained window.

"You'll see. One day you'll be as good a sheep farmer as me and Gran."

"That an order?" Ezra whispered.

"Ayuh."

"Don't have to take orders—from you," Ezra said.

"You will if you know what's good for you."

"Oh, yeah?"

"Yeah," I said.

I walked over and switched the lamp off.

Ezra *would* be alive come spring. He had to be.

 \ *Eleven*

I helped Gran turn and wipe the wheels of sheep's cheese in the ripening cellar beside the house. As I breathed in the faint ammonia smell, my mouth watered.

I liked the slow rhythm of turning milk to cheese.

Gran broke the easy silence. "I got through to Aunt May on the telephone this morning." Aunt May was my father's sister. Gran never held it against her, though, my father leaving my mother and me the way he did. We never talked about him. Aunt May was shamed by what he'd done to us. I guess if I'd wanted to know about him, I could've asked. I didn't want to know.

"How's Bethany?" I said.

Gran looked at me. "A little better. That milk I sent over with Lemmy last week is staying down pretty well. I thought we'd bring a pair of early ewes to them before Christmas. Give the radiation time to settle down at his place a little more. I don't want him coming back here. Must be radiation on his tires still. The readings on the meter rose after he drove up here. I had to wash the road down and sand it."

"Shouldn't we keep the ewes here then?" I asked. "What if they get radioactive over there, the way Uncle Lemmy's cows did, and he has to destroy them, too?"

"Another month, things should be better. Besides, if he keeps the sheep inside his barn and feeds them clean grain and hay, they should do all right. And that'll give 'em fresh milk for Bethany coming in as early as February."

It hurt thinking of Bethany, with her dark eyes and downy hair, so sick.

"Fact is, I'd like to have the whole family come stay here," Gran went on. "Uncle Lemmy won't leave the farm. He says it's all he has. And Aunt May and the cousins won't leave without him. At least having sheep will give him something to do," Gran said.

"What about us? What are we going to do?" I asked.

Gran shrugged. "We'll just keep going. What else? Don't know where we're going to sell all this cheese now Boston's out of the picture. We had our best customers in those fancy shops down there."

"The Harrises can't pay their rent," I told Gran.

"I know."

"What do we do about them?"

"What do you think, girl? You think you just throw people out when hard times hit? They can stay as long as they need to. We've got some money put by. We'll help the Harrises however we can. Same with the Edwards."

The Edwards, a retired couple, rented a house from us too.

"Are our sheep going to be all right?"

"Far as I can tell, Nyle," Gran said. "We'll have everything tested before we sell it, the fleeces, this cheese, the milk, the meat. The wood from the woodlots too. I won't sell anything tainted. But I think our luck held. We still have clean air, clean dirt, clean water. Any release of radiation comes this way, though, the farm could die."

"Like with Aunt May and Uncle Lemmy?"

Gran nodded. Her broad back turned half away.

"Do you like sheep farming, Gran?" I asked.

Gran examined a moldy wheel of cheese. "Wouldn't do it if I didn't."

"What do you like most about it?"

I watched Gran's slow, steady progress down the row. She wiped each wheel of cheese with a cloth soaked in salt brine. She stayed silent so long, I thought she'd forgotten my question.

"That's a hard one, Nyle," she said at last.

"I know." I waited for her to think awhile longer.

"I like the routine," she said.

"I do too."

"And I like being with the sheep."

I nodded. Beads of sweat formed on my forehead and my upper lip in the warm, tangy cellar.

"To be honest, Nyle, there's not much I don't like. Except maybe hoof rot."

"I like the quiet. Inside quiet, outside quiet, you know?"

Gran nodded.

"And I like spring," I said. "When the grass greens up and the lambs come."

"I like that too," said Gran.

"And I like the way the sheep are always there. I like how they never leave."

In the ripening cellar I heard the report of rifle fire. Hunters.

"They're too close," Gran said.

"Ripley, I bet. Probably jacking deer out his bedroom window." I hadn't seen Ripley in some time. He took off school during the three weeks of deer season.

When we finished with the cheese, we changed out of our aprons and boots and climbed up through the bulkhead. Another shot met our ears as the cold air slapped our faces.

Blinded by the brilliant snow, we couldn't see a soul. But from the sound of it, the shot had come from down the hill across the road, behind the flat pasture. Sounded like someone back in the far woodlot. Gran posted only the woods near the sheep and the houses. Normally she went out herself during rifle season and brought home a deer.

"How come you didn't go this year?" I asked, standing outside in the crisp afternoon.

"We're awful close to the contamination zone," Gran said. "What if those deer are grazing on radioactive brush? We can monitor radiation in the feed we give our sheep. But we don't know where or what the deer are browsing. I wouldn't eat that venison."

When I went down the hall to the back bedroom that evening, I found Ezra standing beside his bed. He looked tired and cross, but Mrs. Trent never stopped smiling. Ezra's pajamas hung on his bony shoulders. He'd lost a lot of weight over the last few weeks.

In each hand Ezra gripped the top of a burly-headed cane. Gramp's canes. Gramp had finished carving them in this room, before he got too weak.

Ezra trembled with the effort of holding himself up. His knuckles whitened with exertion.

Mrs. Trent stepped in to help before he collapsed.

"That is enough for today," she said, making Ezra put the canes aside. Before Mrs. Trent went down to the kitchen, she settled Ezra under the covers. His head dropped back and he sighed.

"How are you doing today, Mrs. Trent?" I asked.

"Better, Nyle," Mrs. Trent answered, smiling. "Much better, thank you." Her hair had thinned during her illness, and she'd lost some weight, but she looked stronger as she made her way to the kitchen.

"Hey, Shep," Ezra said. "I'm ready for my lesson—in sheep farming."

"What did you call me?"

"Shep. As in shepherd."

I wondered why he didn't use my real name. "What do you want to know?" I asked.

"First," he said, "why chase those sheep around so much? Mother says you move them—every day."

I smiled. "Not every day. Besides, they don't mind. It's good for them. Until we get the first heavy snow, we rotate them to a fresh section of pasture once or twice a week. It keeps the sheep and the land healthy."

"Sheep rotation?"

"Ayuh. Not a lot of people farm that way in this country. It takes a lot of time. But it works."

I sat down in the flowered chair. I liked talking about the farm. Spreading my legs out in front of me, I rested my hands on my thighs. My socks sagged around my ankles.

Ezra sniffed. "Taken a shower lately?"

"You should talk. You're probably smelling the ripening cellar on my clothes. I've been down with Gran, turning cheese."

"Turning cheese?"

"Gran makes cheese from sheep's milk."

"You milk sheep?"

I bit the inside of my cheek to keep from laughing. "Ayuh, you milk sheep. Not now. We start up after the lambs are born. Spring, summer, through September."

"How are you making cheese now then?"

"We started these wheels last spring. It takes a long time to make cheese."

Ezra picked at a thread on the quilt. "You really don't need the outside world here, do you?"

His question surprised me. Of course we needed the outside world. Without the outside world we had no market, not for the cheese, not for the sheep, or their wool, not even for the timber we took off our land.

"We can do some without the outside world," I said. "But we still need it. What's the good of raising sheep if there's no one to raise them for?"

"Burn your own wood—keeps you warm, cooks your food. Grow fruit. Vegetables. Even make your own cheese. I want that life."

Ezra's eyes smoldered with excitement. As if Gran and I had some secret and he wouldn't rest until we shared it with him.

"Okay," I said. "I won't stop you."

"What do sheep eat after snow comes?" Ezra asked.

"Hay," I said. Just thinking about moving bales in and out of the pickup truck made my back ache.

Ezra shifted in his bed.

"How long to shear a sheep?"

I worried a flap of skin on my thumb. "A few minutes a piece. A few days for all of them."

"All of them?"

I nodded.

"How many?"

"Over three hundred right now. We'll cull some in the spring. We keep most, though."

I answered him and kept answering him until his voice grew hoarse from asking. Occasionally he'd nod off, then wake again. And ask another question.

He hadn't seen any of it, except on the day Gran drove him in. He just heard the workings of the farm coming dimly through the curtained window. That and what we told him.

Ezra put his hands behind his head as I stood to leave. I'd almost stepped into the hallway when I turned and walked back toward him.

"You've been asking me questions all evening, right?"

Ezra nodded.

"Can I ask you one? You can say no if you want. It's a little bit personal."

Ezra looked uneasy.

"It's about the scar over your eye. How did you get that?"

He relaxed. Maybe he'd thought I'd ask about the accident. He didn't know me very well if he thought I'd bring that up.

"I was maybe five years old," Ezra said, smiling. "Jumping on the bed one night. Mother warned me not to."

I looked at Ezra, imagining him as a five-year-old.

"My mother fell apart when she saw all the blood. It was

my father who carried me to the doctor's house across the road."

Could it be only a few days ago I thought the room would win again, that Ezra would die?

"Know what, Shep?" Ezra said. "I feel like that bird. The phoenix. It burns up, then rises from its ashes."

I listened, watching him. I'd never heard of a bird like that, but now I wouldn't likely forget it.

"Feels good to be alive, Shep," Ezra said.

I eyed the canes with the burly handles leaning against the wall beside the bed. Gramp's canes. I'd cut the wood with him. I'd watched him strip the bark, shape the canes, sand them, oil them.

Gramp was gone.

But Ezra was still here.

 *Twelve*

November slid into December. Ezra grew stronger, though he still needed Gramp's canes.

I would come down the hall calling, "Hey, Ezra. I hope you're decent."

"All depends on what you mean by decent," Ezra would answer, waggling his eyebrow.

Ezra asked about school, about the weather, about how things smelled outside.

I worried he might make himself sick again. He pushed so hard, hobbling back and forth across the wide floorboards of his room. Sometimes he got up every hour, other times he lay in bed, unable to find the strength to go on.

I wondered that he didn't drive Mrs. Trent out of her mind. She always left the room when I came, heading to the bathroom for a shower, or to the kitchen for a visit with Gran.

I also wondered why Ezra made his trips back and forth but never left the room.

But I didn't spend much time worrying about that. At least I knew where to find him.

Gran took most of my weekly chores. She said, "The days are too short for you to be of any use after school." So she shouldered the bulk of the farm work and I spent more time with Ezra.

On weekends, though, Gran did paperwork, milking and lambing records, and I did the chores.

The barn needed mucking out, the manure piled for composting. Back and forth on the tractor. I'd put a week or so into it already. I had another two or three weeks of work to go.

Sometimes Muncie tagged along with me. Then, when all the work was done, she'd come up with an idea to hold me longer, like sledding in the front pasture, or snowball fights. Anything that kept me out with her.

Afterward I would come to Ezra's room red-cheeked, smelling of snow and wet wool. Striding down the hall, I felt a smile unfold inside me like a new leaf.

One Saturday Muncie trundled down and rushed me through chores. The night before, five inches of fresh clean snow had fallen. Perfect packing snow. In the distance the blue sky stretched over rolling waves of white.

When we finished with the sheep, Muncie dragged her boot across the field beside the steep front pasture, dividing it into two halves. Caleb sat at my side, his tail wagging a fan-shaped pattern in the snow.

"First we build forts," Muncie said. "Choose your weapon."

Muncie held up a hollow plastic block for making snow bricks in one hand, and a sand pail in the other.

I chose the snow brick.

Then Muncie and I stood on the dividing line back to back, and Muncie counted ten paces. Her voice echoed down the valley.

Caleb danced around us, springing up in the air and butting me with his nose. Our boots crunched in the snow as Muncie and I paced away from each other. Here I had the advantage: my legs stretched longer. I could get farther from the line than Muncie. But Muncie had the stronger pitching arm.

Every now and then I'd look up toward the house and wonder about Ezra. I almost wished the curtain would open, even with Muncie there, but the curtain stayed closed.

Muncie built her fort quickly. That girl did everything fast. As soon as her fortress wall was up, she slunk behind it and started packing snowballs. Caleb barked and tunneled his nose into the snow, throwing snoutfuls up in the air.

I checked on Muncie's progress every few minutes, working furiously to catch up with her.

"You're going to eat ice, Nyle Sumner," Muncie called, still wearing her radiation mask.

Hard as I tried to catch up, my fort had to be higher because of my size. Muncie ended up throwing the first snowball of the battle.

"Foul!" I cried, leaving my work on the fort and pounding a snowball into shape. "I wasn't ready."

Caleb raced around the field, his bark echoing through the crisp air.

I ducked behind my wall as another of Muncie's snowballs whistled toward me.

Clumps of snow stuck to my mittens as I mashed and shaped snowball after snowball. I surveyed Muncie's fort, found the weakest point, and pounded it until I'd knocked it down. Caleb jumped over the collapsed wall, barking at Muncie.

Muncie, without any more protection, came forward, closer to the line, trying to score on me. She got my fort down in spite of my efforts to drive her back.

By afternoon, we both dripped—outside as well as inside our winter clothes.

"I surrender," I said.

Muncie crossed her arms over her snowsuit and gloated.

We brushed the worst of the snow off each other and started up toward home, Caleb leading the way. I heard Ripley yelling for Tyrus somewhere back on his property. We stopped in the field and stared in the direction of the shouts.

Within moments Ripley emerged from the woods.

Caleb came and sat, alert, at my feet.

Red Jackson had warned Ripley to keep Tyrus on a chain after the last sheep kill. He'd said we'd be in our rights to shoot Tyrus if he came after our sheep again. Red swore he'd stop Tyrus for good the next time he saw him loose. But either Ripley didn't pay attention, or he didn't have any control over that dog, because it looked like Tyrus had slipped him again.

"You seen my dog?" Ripley yelled.

I shook my head. "How long has he been missing?"

"Since last night," Ripley said.

I'd checked all the pastures this morning and there'd been

no sign of trouble. I worried about the sheep with Tyrus on the loose.

Muncie, standing a little ways behind, bent down, shaped a snowball, and lobbed it toward me. I dodged and the snowball sailed across the road to land near Ripley's feet.

"You two want to fight?" Ripley yelled, forming a snowball of his own.

"What'd you do that for?" I whispered to Muncie.

Slam! Before I knew what was happening, Ripley's snowball zipped past me and hit Muncie right in the stomach. Her breath popped out of her like a lamb suddenly born. Muncie doubled over. Caleb ran to her and whined.

"Ripley!" I yelled.

I ran over to Muncie. "You okay?"

Muncie nodded, unable to speak. The material of her snowsuit rubbed against itself, making a nylon song.

Another snowball sailed out of Ripley's hand and smashed against my leg. The hair rose on Caleb's back and every muscle tensed.

"Cut it out!" I yelled at Ripley.

"Cut it out," he mimicked.

Caleb growled. The sound carried in the cold air.

Ripley took a step back. He transferred a snowball from one hand to the other, but he didn't throw it. "You see my dog, you let me know."

"I'll let you know, all right."

Keeping my arm around Muncie, I helped her to the road, guiding her to the tire tracks. Walking on the packed snow made easier going.

Gradually Muncie straightened up.

"Why'd you throw a snowball at him, Munce?"

"I didn't. I was aiming at you."

"Muncie, you've got lousy aim."

"You ducked! I thought if we ignored him, if we were busy with each other, he'd go away—"

Caleb had run ahead, almost to the barn, but Muncie stopped. I turned to look at her. She was staring at my house.

The sun had set and shadows gathered on the trampled snow. Gran had switched on the houselights, inside and out. A rosy glow filled the late afternoon. At this angle Ezra's room showed just beyond the shed.

And the curtain to Ezra's room stood open.

I had hoped for this, and yet a feeling of dread knotted inside me.

Two figures filled the tall bedroom window, easily seen in the growing darkness. While his mother hovered beside him, Ezra gazed out the window, a mask covering his nose and mouth.

"Who are they?" Muncie asked.

I looked back over my shoulder toward Ripley's property. No sign of him. At least Ripley hadn't seen them.

I turned back as the curtain slid shut.

Muncie shivered beside me. "Who were they?"

"Come on," I said. "You're cold. I'll walk you home."

"You're not going to tell me who they were, are you?" Muncie said, stomping the snow off her boots in her mud-room. "Are you?"

The weight of my wet snow clothes dragged at me.

"Well, until you have something to say to me," Muncie said, fury prickling her voice, "I don't have anything to say to you, either."

I shivered as I crunched back down the road toward

home. The shadow of woods and hills darkened my path.
Partly I shivered with nervousness, that Muncie had seen
Ezra. I shivered with excitement, too, seeing him like that
myself.

Gran had pale coffee waiting on the kitchen table for me.

"I saw Ezra at the window."

Gran nodded.

"I'll go down to his room as soon as I change," I said,
kicking off my wet clothes and tearing up to my room.

My legs ached, my feet stung, my stomach nearly
shriveled with hunger, and I had to pee. I hurriedly stripped
down and pulled on some dry clothes. I glanced at my
stinging face in the mirror.

"Nyle?" Gran called.

Gran stood at the bottom of the steps, her spotted hand
resting on the door frame. She looked up toward me, her hair
mashed under her net.

"I'll be right there," I called. Back at the mirror, I tried
brushing the static out of my hair—making it worse.

Ezra wouldn't die. Even he believed it now. Really believed it. He'd opened the curtain.

I heard heavy breathing coming up behind me and imagined for just one moment I'd turn and see Ezra.

Gran stood at the top of the steps in the doorway to my
bedroom. The smell of coffee clung to her. I remembered the
steaming mug, waiting downstairs on the kitchen table.

"Nyle?" Gran asked.

I glowered at my reflection. My hair crackled with static.
How could I go see Ezra looking like a helicopter head?

Gran sat down beside Bayley on the window seat, the
window seat Gramp had built for me.

I didn't have time for one of our talks. I wanted to get downstairs. I grabbed a book. "Not now, Gran."

"Right now," Gran said.

I lay the book on my dresser.

"Ezra's getting better."

"So how come I can't go see him?"

"You can. Just not yet."

I sat on the edge of my bed and faced Gran. Bayley jumped off the window seat and padded over, leaping up next to me. He climbed into my lap, made a wobbly circle, and finally curled up.

Gran shifted. "How do you feel about Ezra?"

I held very still. "I wasn't happy about his coming here in the beginning."

Gran nodded.

"It was the room that worried me."

"And it doesn't worry you anymore?"

I thought about how much I loved going to his room. It had become Ezra's room. Even though Mrs. Trent slept there, even though it had always been the back bedroom before. I realized I thought of it now as Ezra's room.

"You two getting friendly?"

I shrugged.

"Too friendly?"

"Gran, are you going to give me 'the talk'?"

"You've been around sheep long enough, you don't need that talk, do you?"

Moonlight washed across Gran's shoulders.

"I wouldn't mind hearing you give it."

"Maybe some other time. Nyle, what I want to say is, he's going to leave sometime. You understand that. We can ask them to go now, before you two get any closer. He's strong enough. They could leave anytime."

"Can't we afford to keep them?"

"That's not it. As long as we can take care of ourselves, we'll take care of them, too."

"Then what? Where could they go, Gran? You said they don't have anybody."

Gran sat on the window seat, watching me.

"Nyle, death isn't the only kind of leaving that hurts."

I stroked the cat and tried blocking out what Gran was saying. "I know." For an instant I thought about my father. "I know that. Gran, I only want Ezra to get better."

"Good," Gran said. "Then listen. The visiting nurse says Ezra needs to leave that room. He's a fifteen-year-old boy. He needs to get out."

I remembered, with all his exercising on Gramp's canes, how Ezra never crossed the threshold into the hallway. Mrs. Trent still carried a bedpan back and forth to the bathroom for him.

I'd been afraid to go into that room. Ezra was afraid to leave it. "Outside frightens him," I said.

"We know. But he took the first step by opening the curtain today. He only let us do that after listening to you and Muncie whooping it up out there all afternoon. And then only after we'd checked every square inch of the window with the radiation detector. He insisted on wearing a mask, though the readings showed clean. I'm glad you didn't throw yours away, Nyle. So, next we get him out."

"What if he leaves the room and gets sick again?" Mr. Sobel said radiation damage accumulated in the body. He said the body couldn't repair the molecules and cell parts already harmed. And each exposure destroyed more.

"Nyle, I've stopped checking radiation levels here. Everything in the house is clean. He won't get sicker."

"Could you put that in writing?" I asked.

"Wouldn't mean a thing if I did," Gran said. "There are no guarantees in this life. You know that."

I did.

In the last month everything had changed. Everywhere around, little things, big things changed, as the effects of the accident reached North Haversham. Finding safe food and water, getting hold of money, finding substitute teachers to replace the ones who hadn't come back. Rationing gasoline, finding heating oil, stretching cooking fuel.

But with Ezra, the changes were good. Slowly he shook off the symptoms of radiation sickness. He was getting better, growing stronger.

I pushed all my worries down inside where I wouldn't have to think about them. Only Ezra mattered. And Ezra was getting better.

 \ *Thirteen*

I often found Ezra lying back on his bed, exhausted. I knew Gran and Mrs. Trent helped him plenty during the day while I sat through endless hours at school. But they were waiting for me to move him out of that room, and I couldn't find the right way to do it.

One night Ezra looked particularly tired.

"I can't stay long," I said.

"A lot of homework?" Ezra asked.

"In a way. I'm going out to watch a meteor shower. It's a class assignment."

"Meteor shower this time of year?"

"They mostly happen during the summer, but my science teacher said to look for one tonight."

"You'll tell me about it tomorrow," Ezra said. "Eh, Shep?"

He had perked up a little, looked interested.

"You could see it yourself."

"Sure, I could." Ezra sounded excited. "I could watch it out the window."

I shrugged. "Not the same out the window."

"Ah," Ezra said. "One of those purists, are you?"

"No. I thought you might like seeing it. Really seeing it. Outside. You can't see much of anything from this window."

"You'd be surprised," Ezra said.

"No. I think you'd be."

Ezra swept his curls off his forehead. "You don't think I can leave this room, do you?"

I looked down at my stockinged feet.

Ezra threw his blankets aside, stood, grabbed the canes, and barreled toward the doorway. The gauze mask hanging from the dresser mirror swung as he passed. But at the entrance to the room he stopped.

Ezra stood, hesitating. The veins throbbed in his neck.

You can do it, Ezra, I thought, willing him to take one more step.

But he couldn't. His fear held him back. He knew any more radiation exposure could be lethal. He'd taken such a high dose. Only a little more could kill him.

Ezra wanted to live. He wanted it too much to risk leaving the safety of the room. This room, which had been the death room to Gramp and to my mother, offered the only hope of life to Ezra.

Slowly Ezra turned and limped back to his bed. He threw the canes down with a clatter and collapsed, defeated, onto the quilt. He wouldn't look at me again.

Outside in the biting dark, halfway up the road to Muncie's house, bundled in my wool clothes, I scanned the night sky for shooting stars. At least the nuclear accident couldn't meddle with this.

The fine white dust of a star chased across the sky over Ripley's land.

The cry of coydogs on the ridge startled the clear, cold night. Caleb whined at my side.

With Tyrus on the loose and the threat of winter-hungry coyotes, I had plenty reason to worry about the sheep. "Ripley's right," I told Caleb. "We do need another guard dog."

A dog to guard the sheep. It could be Ezra's dog. I remembered the first night of Ezra's stay with us, how I squatted in the hallway. The light from the bathroom stole over my shoulder to touch the curly-headed boy in the dying bed. I remembered his words: "I had a dog." Maybe time had come for him to have a dog again.

I shivered outside in the frigid night, watching another meteor streak across the sky. I imagined Ezra bounding through the pastures, a Great Pyrenees at his side.

"Ezra'd get along great with a dog like that," I told Caleb. "They have so much in common—they're both stubborn. And it's hard to say who has the bigger feet."

That weekend Gran drove me in the truck up north, the back way, to Holland Farm. Mrs. Holland said they'd felt the effects of the Cookshire accident too. No radiation, but everything delivered to the area had to come from the north or the west. The government had shut the southern route down.

We bought the last male in the litter. Mrs. Holland led us out to the barn where we found him packed in with the sheep.

I held the fat, fuzzy mop of a puppy on my lap the whole

way home. Over and over I stroked his little bearlike head. Playing with the droopy ears, I breathed in the rubber smell of his puppyness. I imagined how Ezra'd feel having a new dog. The puppy's almond-shaped eyes reminded me of Ezra.

Mrs. Trent smiled and clapped her hands when she saw the puppy. "How wonderful."

Ezra sat up in bed reading a book I'd borrowed for him. I had the puppy stashed under my sweater. It kept squirming.

Must have been a good book. Ezra hardly noticed me at first. I stood at the entrance of his room, waiting. Finally he surfaced, took a second look. His full lips opened into a smile.

"What have you got?"

"Come and find out," I said.

Ezra's eyebrows shot up, disappearing under his curls. "You want me to check what you have under your sweater, Shep?"

I blushed, quickly pulling the puppy out. "He's for you," I said.

I expected—I don't know what I'd expected. At least that he'd like the dog.

But Ezra's smile left his face. "What do you mean bringing him in here?"

"He's a present," I said. "For you. From me and Gran."

Ezra's face took on a haunted look. "Get it out of here. Get it out!"

"Ezra, what's the matter?"

"Take it away!"

His voice shrilled.

"Ezra, what's wrong with you!" He frightened me.

"Get it out!" Ezra screamed. "Get it out!"

Pressing the puppy to my chest, I ran blindly from his room into the kitchen.

Holding the dog close, I tried to stop shaking.

Gran fixed up a box. She folded an old towel into the bottom and placed the makeshift dog bed by the stove.

The puppy should have spent the night with Ezra.

In another month it'd be out all the time. Guard dogs belonged outside, with the sheep. The cold and the puppy's size would keep it inside for a while, but that couldn't last forever.

I'd thought it'd be perfect, that puppy spending a month of nights alongside Ezra. They'd be ready to go out together, I'd thought, Ezra and the dog.

The puppy chewed a piece of cardboard dangling inside the box. He chewed and batted at the soggy paper with one large paw, then flopped down and fell asleep.

In the morning I led the puppy down to the flat pasture to spend the day with a flock of the older ewes. Out of the corner of my eye I noticed Ezra's curtain open. "I hope you're watching," I said under my breath as the puppy rolled and tumbled down the road. Muncie noticed the puppy, but she didn't ask about it. She'd been keeping her distance ever since she saw Ezra in the window.

That afternoon I got off the school bus and crossed over to the flat pasture. The puppy bounded through the field and flung himself against my legs. He tugged at my bootlaces. I tended the sheep, then brought the puppy up the hill with me toward home.

"You taking the pup in to Ezra again tonight?" Gran asked.

I dangled a piece of old clothesline in front of the puppy. He swaggered up and barked at it. A high puppy bark.

I shrugged.

"Do it," Gran said.

So when I visited Ezra that night, the puppy came too. I pulled a little wool cap over his head and fastened a bell around his thick neck.

Down on the floor of Ezra's room, the puppy staggered under the weight of the hat. He knocked it off his head and onto the floor. The puppy took the hat in his teeth and dragged it around Ezra's room. Lugging it along sideways, occasionally he'd trip over it and roll. His collar jingled with each step. He dropped the hat beside Ezra's bed and started sniffing.

"He's going to pee in here," Ezra said.

"No he's not." I refused to let Ezra rattle me tonight.

"I'm telling you he's going to pee in here." Ezra sounded close to panic. "I know when a dog is going to pee. Don't let him. Please don't let him!"

"Why are you so upset? If he pees, he pees. Puppies do that. I'll clean it up." Such a stupid way to act. It made me furious. "Maybe I should put him on the bed," I said. "Let him pee on you."

"No!" Ezra cried.

I scooped the puppy off the floor and, hesitating only a moment, dropped him on top of Ezra. "Why not?"

Ezra sat staring at the dog. The dog stood up, wobbled, and stared back at Ezra.

"He's a good dog, Ezra," I said.

Ezra sat, frozen.

At that moment the puppy squatted and peed.

"Oh God!" Ezra cried. He smacked the puppy off the bed with his hand. The puppy squealed, landed on the floor.

It started whimpering.

"Listen to it," Ezra screamed. "It's sick. You put a sick dog on me."

Ezra struggled to throw the blankets off him. "You don't know. You don't know how radioactive this dog is."

"Radioactive?"

Mrs. Trent ran to the room.

"It could kill me. Radiation in its pee could kill me!"

"It couldn't, Ezra." He wasn't making any sense.

I gathered up the puppy and started talking softly. I tried calming it, calming myself.

"It's all right. Look. He's not radioactive. He can't be radioactive. We got him up north. Far north. He's clean."

Ezra's face quivered in horror. He wasn't listening to me. He'd skidded beyond hearing. Mrs. Trent stepped forward in her shabby, ill-fitting clothes. I cut in front of her.

"Ezra. The puppy's not sick. You surprised him, that's all. He cried out because you surprised him. Listen, he only pees on people he likes. You don't think he pees on just anybody, do you?"

Ezra was out of his bed, shivering in the corner of the room, leaning against the wall for support.

I brought the puppy closer to him. Ezra shrank into himself.

"He's dying of radiation," Ezra cried. "He's dying."

I'd lost my patience. "There's nothing wrong with this dog!" I yelled. "No radioactivity, no poison, no nothing. Just a normal puppy. Look, Ezra."

"Get it away!" Ezra screamed, flinging his arms up to cover his face. "Get it away from me."

"What about the damn bird you told me about?" I cried. "That phoenix you said you were. You're not rising out of any ashes now."

Ezra stared at his bare feet, his bare blue feet. His blood still slogged too slowly through his body. Unable to hold himself up any longer, he collapsed into a heap on the floor.

"Don't bring me anything to love," he whispered. "I don't want anything to love." Ezra hid his face.

Mrs. Trent knelt beside her son, helping him up. Dark circles shadowed her eyes. She struggled to lift Ezra and put him back to bed.

"Not there," he cried. "Not that bed."

Mrs. Trent guided Ezra across to her cot. "Would you leave us now, please, Nyle?" she said.

"Fine!" I screamed. "Just fine."

I gathered the puppy in my arms, turned my back on the Trents, and stormed out of the room.

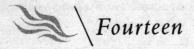 \ *Fourteen*

I heard voices downstairs in the kitchen, voices drifting through the grate as I lay in bed that night. Women's voices reaching through the floor to me, Gran and Mrs. Trent. They'd become friends in these last weeks. They had nothing in common, would never have noticed the other under ordinary circumstances, but these were not ordinary circumstances. They had made a connection.

Pulling a pillow over my head, I chose not to listen to them. But still I saw them in my mind—talking over steaming cups of coffee, leaning softly toward each other. Gran and Mrs. Trent, their voices rose and fell like the singing of cicadas.

The next morning Gran stood at the stove, scraping the spatula across the cast-iron skillet, frying up eggs.

"I'm driving you to Manchester after chores today," she said.

"Manchester?"

"I have sheep business there this morning. You can get your Christmas shopping done. I'll come back and pick you up around six."

What shopping we did, we usually did in Cookshire. Even though North Haversham lay halfway between the two towns, the roads into Cookshire made for easier driving. And Cookshire offered a wider variety of stores. But now there was no Cookshire. How could there still be a Christmas?

"What about Ezra?"

Gran kept frying eggs, ignoring my question.

I sliced a piece of sharp cheese and nibbled at it.

"If we're heading for Manchester today, could Muncie come?" I hoped to smooth things out between us—if she'd even go. I wasn't sure she'd go.

"Ask her," Gran said.

Manchester sparkled in its silvery wrappings. A mantle of snow outlined the trees and buildings. Tinsel garlands ran from streetlamp to streetlamp. Ropes of evergreens snaked around window fronts and door frames.

In the window of the Northshire Bookstore, a plastic Santa wore a gauze mask. Several shoppers wore masks too. At least Muncie wouldn't be the only one in a mask today.

Muncie had agreed to come, but she squeezed herself so close against the door on the way to Manchester, I worried about her falling out. After Gran left us, though, she warmed up and started acting herself.

Stepping up to a sparkling shop window, I leaned closer to take it all in. An angel was spinning jerkily at the top of a beribboned Christmas tree.

"Look, Nyle," Muncie said. She spun on her short,

bowed legs on the slushy sidewalk, imitating the angel. She would have just fit in that window display, too.

I laughed with Muncie.

A few girls from school caught up to us, said hello, and then moved on. It surprised me, seeing them. I didn't know anyone from North Haversham who shopped in Manchester before the accident.

Muncie and I stayed an arm's length apart, tromping through the crowded streets. We clomped inside stores, walked around sale tables, then headed out into the cold again.

Near lunchtime Muncie motioned me inside a coffee shop. We stood in the doorway a moment while our eyes adjusted to the dim light of the restaurant.

Muncie and I took the first available table and sat down opposite each other.

"She's a little thing," the waitress said. She meant Muncie. The waitress flipped her pad open. "Is she one of those, what do ya call 'em?"

"Dwarves?" Muncie suggested.

Still the waitress spoke only to me. "She could work this time of year as Santa's little helper. Maybe she is Santa's little helper. On a coffee break."

She laughed at her own joke.

I sat there, embarrassed for Muncie. Why did people treat her that way—as if she had no feelings, as if she weren't even there?

"Can you tell me where the bathroom is?" Muncie asked.

Instead of answering, the waitress pinched Muncie's cheek through the mask and told me how cute she was. "The bathroom's around that corner," she told me. "Right next to the kitchen."

My heart hammered against my ribs.

Muncie's pale eyes sparked with anger, her eyebrows shot up above the top of her glasses. She stared for a moment at the waitress, then got up and walked toward the bathroom.

I should have defended her. Why didn't I stand up for her?

Muncie returned, calm. She'd already let the whole thing with the waitress go.

"Did you see this?" I asked. There was a notice on each table: ALL FOOD AND WATER SERVED IN THIS RESTAURANT IS RADIATION FREE.

I almost said how Ezra would like that. But I caught myself.

While we sipped cocoa and ate sandwiches, Dan Taylor and three other boys from our eighth-grade class burst through the restaurant door.

Muncie wrinkled her nose under her mask.

"There goes the neighborhood," she said, loud enough for the boys to hear.

Dan tipped his fedora and smiled.

They bantered with us, waiting for a table to open. The one beside ours cleared first.

Muncie ate as fast as she did everything else. Once finished, she grabbed a packet of sweetener from a bowl on the table. Muncie launched the packet at me like a paper football, using her index finger as the kicker. Muncie and her crummy aim, each time she flicked the packet it went a little wilder. On the fifth try the packet soared over my head and landed on the floor beside the boys' table.

Dan leaned over and picked up the sweetener packet. Tearing it open, he poured the powder into his water glass. He stirred the mixture, took a swallow. "Ahhh," he said, smacking his lips together.

All the boys snatched sweetener packets and copied Dan.

"Does this mean you're all sweet on me?" Muncie asked.

Except for Dan, all the boys pushed their water glasses away.

But Dan Taylor held his hat on his head with one hand and leaned forward in his chair with an exaggerated bow, first to Muncie, then to me.

Muncie and I went into a huddle. It was the closest she'd come to me all day.

"I think Dan likes you," she said.

"You're crazy." I took a bite of my pickle.

"I'm not—"

A pink sweetener packet landed on the tablecloth between us.

"Isn't anybody sweet on me?" Dan asked.

Muncie got a know-it-all look on her face.

I picked up the pink packet. Without looking, I tossed it back over my shoulder toward the boys' table. It landed with a plunk in Dan's water glass.

"Great shot, Sumner," Dan said. "Three points."

"Three points for Sumner," the boys echoed.

My cheeks went hot. I liked Dan. Not as a boyfriend, just liked him. He was funny. Like Ezra.

At the next table one of the boys gave a phony cough. Suddenly pink packets, dozens of them, rained down onto Muncie's and my heads.

The waitress shouted, "You kids. Cut it out."

"Yeah," Muncie said. "Cut it out, you kids."

"Hey, dwarf, why don't you run back to your cottage and fetch your seven little brothers," one of the boys said.

Dan hit the boy in the arm.

"Let's go," I told Muncie.

We paid our bill and left.

By the end of the day I'd had enough of Christmas shopping. I'd had enough of being in town. We planned to meet Gran outside Radio Shack at six fifteen. We had fifteen minutes to kill.

"Let's wait inside," I said. "You're shivering out here."

Inside Radio Shack, rows and rows of television sets were turned on, tuned to the local station. No sound, just the same picture, repeated thirty times on the various-sized screens.

As we stood and watched, the local newscasters sat behind a desk, soundlessly introducing the first story.

They ran a film clip showing one side of the Cookshire plant blown open. A blackened, ragged hole filled the screens. Twisted chunks of debris spewed across the ground. Helicopters passed above with monitoring equipment, measuring the radiation release from the containment building. All around the site emergency firefighters scrambled, wearing suits like astronauts wear.

The next film showed New Hampshire traffic jams. People fought, children hid under blankets in the backseats of abandoned cars. We'd seen that clip at school.

Then they panned across stretches of land, showing aerial views of the evacuated cities and towns: mile upon mile empty of life. Everything looked perfectly normal, just empty. An orange wind sock flapped above the unplowed runways at Logan Airport. The streets of Boston's business district stood empty.

But not completely empty. Packs of dogs, looking thin and dangerous, stalked up and down the avenues, weaving in and out between the abandoned cars. Shoulder to shoulder they scavenged, occasionally turning on each other.

They showed a crowded evacuation center, a hospital with patients on the floors, bodies in a temporary morgue. Men weeping. A child, wide-eyed, under a clear plastic tent.

Other people gathered around us in the store.

The head of the Nuclear Regulatory Commission appeared, identified by a flash of words under his face.

Then the President of the United States came on.

Finally the camera returned to a somber-faced anchorwoman.

And then they cut to a string of commercials, idiotic commercials.

Muncie tugged at my arm and turned me away from the television screens.

Gran planned on meeting us outside at six fifteen. We were late.

 \ *Fifteen*

With her one-pot mentality, Gran rarely thought of making anything but oatmeal or fried eggs for breakfast. I hated oatmeal and I wasn't crazy about fried eggs. As soon as I was old enough to use the stove, I learned to make pancakes.

Since the accident, food could be hard to get. Especially fresh eggs and milk. Between what Gran had canned and frozen, and the general store in North Haversham, we usually found things to eat. Almost everything at the store came in tins now and cost twice as much as it had before. What you needed wasn't always there. But so far no one had starved to death.

The Sunday after our trip to Manchester, I steamed a large pan of apples with honey and cinnamon. I fried pancakes in the shape of sheep. Dozens of cakey, golden-brown lambs leaping from the pan onto the warming plate.

Gran never made frivolous food, but I knew she liked eating it. She'd put down a huge plate of my pancakes.

I tipped the bowl and scraped the last spoonfuls of raw batter as Gran came in from outside. The puppy looked up from inside his box, sniffing hopefully, then flopped his head back down.

Drizzling the last of the batter into the hot skillet, I listened as pancake sheep sizzled. The cinnamon apple smell warmed the kitchen.

I hadn't seen Ezra in more than twenty-four hours.

Gran poured herself some coffee. She sat at the table, her hands wrapped around the steaming mug. She studied a pile of papers. They'd come in the mail yesterday from the government—new regulations for dairy sheep. A lot of cows supplying milk to this area had died because of the accident. Clean little farms like ours suddenly interested the government.

"It's bitter out there this morning," Gran said. "Better not put the puppy out yet."

I never minded his staying in.

"Gran?" I said, watching the pancakes. "I've been thinking about Ezra and his mother staying on. Even after he's all better."

Gran turned her face to me, a cloud of steam softening her features. She took a sip of coffee. Shook her head. "They can't."

"Why not?" I looked over at her.

"Nyle, we're part of the accident. Ezra and his mother need a fresh start."

"What will happen to them?"

Gran snapped at me. "Pay attention to what you're doing. You're scorching your sheep, girl."

I slid the spatula under the sheep pancakes and flipped them. The undersides had blackened.

"Ezra likes the farm," I said. "At least he likes hearing about it. I know he'd like to stay."

"He'd love to stay. Right in that back room," Gran said. "That doesn't mean that's what's best for him."

"How do *you* know what's best for him?"

Gran got up and brought butter and maple syrup to the table. Our neighbors, the Hulls, made our syrup. What about this year? Would they boil sap? Would it be safe to eat? I brought the pancakes and steamed apples to the table and sat down.

"Gran, how can you even think about letting Ezra leave?" I forked a stack of pancake sheep onto my plate. "He's the first person I ever met who likes your cooking."

Gran buttered her sheep. "He's not paying me any compliments. Fifteen-year-old boys eat anything."

I took a mouthful of sticky pancakes.

"Thirteen-year-old girls, too," Gran said, watching me shovel in my stack of sheep.

"Muncie would rather starve than eat your cooking."

"I don't have to listen to this. Unless you want to start fixing all the meals."

"Would you eat pancakes three times a day?"

Gran cackled.

She got up to pour herself more coffee, nearly tripping over Bayley sprawled across the linoleum. "Darn cat. Always underfoot."

"Gran!" I picked Bayley up. We used to let him out anytime he asked. But I worried about his eating contaminated mice, and so we kept him in most of the time now.

"Forgive me," Gran said. "His royal mouse catcher deserves to sleep anywhere he pleases, even if he has to trip an old woman to do it."

I poured some spicy apple slices onto Gran's plate. "Sit down and eat," I ordered.

Gran slathered butter over a line of sheep, then covered the pancakes with spiced apples. "We got Ezra to come out yesterday while you were gone."

I sagged in my chair. "I wanted to bring him out."

"You did," Gran said. "He did it to prove to you he could."

Gran cut off the head of a pancake sheep. She speared an apple with her fork, popped the mess into her mouth, and chewed. "Nyle, you better eat your sheep before Caleb comes along and drives them onto my plate."

Between the two of us, every pancake disappeared, even the blackened ones, except a few I set aside for Ezra. I used my finger to wipe up the last of the spicy apple juice from my plate.

As Gran cleared the table, a commotion sounded in the hallway.

It was Ezra. He was coming toward the kitchen.

"Go help them," Gran said. "I'll bring Caleb out and get the sheep loaded to take to Lemmy's."

"What about chores?"

"Done already," Gran said.

I suddenly felt shy and embarrassed, after the scene with the dog the other night. Ezra wouldn't want me to come down the hall to help. I busied myself cleaning the kitchen instead.

"Do you like our surprise, Nyle?" Mrs. Trent asked from the hallway.

I turned toward her. Her eyes looked fresh and bright, like she'd slept well. The circles under her lower lids weren't nearly so dark, and Gran had found her a nicer dress to wear.

She turned back toward Ezra. "Almost there."

As he entered the kitchen, the part of his face visible above the mask showed red with effort. A fine film of sweat formed on his temples. In each hand Ezra gripped one of Gramp's canes. His white knuckles jutted over the well-rubbed brown of the walking sticks.

"Nyle is cleaning the kitchen," Mrs. Trent said, stating the obvious. "Nyle, I will ask you to close the curtains." She lifted her hand to tuck some hair behind an ear. Her hand was shaking.

I wanted to tell her, to tell them both, there was no danger, no radiation to harm them. But I didn't want to ruin things. I pulled the curtains shut.

"Only a few more steps to the table, Ezra," Mrs. Trent said. "You are almost there."

Ezra labored past his mother on the canes, his face tight with effort.

"I am going back to tidy our room, Ezra," Mrs. Trent said.

She stood for a moment, unsure whether or not to leave. Finally she eased past Ezra, heading down the hall.

Ezra rested on the two canes and lifted his head. His eyes swept over the kitchen: the double sink, the woodstove, my outside clothes hanging over chairs in front of the hearth. He took in the enamel coffee pot, the doorless cabinets stacked with dishes and cans and preserves, the large oak table. He avoided looking at the outside door and the curtained windows.

"How you doing, Ezra?" I asked, standing at the sink.

Ezra didn't answer. He studied the room suspiciously, as if something waited in hiding.

I concentrated on my dishwashing.

"Where's the dog?" Ezra asked.

"Caleb? He's out with Gran."

"I meant the other one."

"The puppy? He's over there in the box by the stove, sleeping off breakfast. Gran said it was too cold to put him out yet this morning."

Ezra made his way over to the table and dropped into a chair. "The puppy spends all day outside?"

I nodded. "His job is to guard sheep. Pretty soon he'll spend all night outside too."

Ezra stared across the table toward the box. "Is this room safe?" he asked. "Has anyone measured the radiation in here today?"

"Perfectly safe," I said, drying my hands on the backs of my jeans. "No radiation anywhere."

I picked up the detector and swept it around the room. It crackled innocently.

"Oh, wait," I said. "Maybe a general inspection isn't enough for you." I waved the detector under the sink, inside the cabinets, under my armpit, over the stove, over the box with the puppy inside. The detector ticked its note of safety.

When I got near the box with the puppy, Ezra shifted in his seat to get a better look.

"Hey," I called down to the box.

The puppy scrambled to his feet and whined.

I scooped him up out of his box. "We've got to check you, too."

Lifting his ear, I slid the wand underneath. The soft crackle annoyed him. He shook his head and sneezed, trying to grab the detector in his mouth and chew on it. The puppy squirmed, his paws paddling air to get away. I aimed the detector at his fuzzy rear end.

"You won't find any radiation there," Ezra said in disgust.

"You don't know how dangerous these puppies can be," I said. "You think they're okay and then they go and pee radiation all over you."

"There's no radiation in that dog," Ezra said.

"Maybe you're right. Doesn't seem to be any radiation in this whole kitchen. You could take off that mask if you wanted. Eat some of these pancakes I saved for you." I waved the detector over the plate. "See, they're clean."

"No, thanks."

Ezra placed Gramp's canes across his lap. He ran his hand up and down the surface of the table. "I'll just leave the mask on. I'm not too hungry right now anyway."

I sat across from Ezra at the kitchen table. I'd never sat at this table with a boy before. I'd never even seen Ezra in a chair. It felt funny, dancey sort of, having him across from me like that. I guess I smiled.

Ezra spread his large hands out, leaned toward me, and smiled back.

"Welcome to the land of the living, Ezra Trent," I said, stroking the puppy in my lap.

A cloud passed over his face, sudden. Then it was gone.

"Sure I can't get you something to eat?"

Ezra looked around the kitchen again, this time without
fear or suspicion. The woodstove radiated waves of heat. Ezra
studied the wood box, the old round-edged refrigerator, the
sinks stained orange with minerals. He turned back to me
and reached toward the dog.

"What's the matter? Afraid he'll pee on me?" I asked.

"Serve you right if he did," Ezra answered.

Gran came in just then, letting in a blast of cold wind,
stomping snow off her boots.

"Nyle. I'll need your help getting that pair of ewes over
to Aunt May and Uncle Lemmy's. Oh, and bring the puppy
out too. He can go down in the front pasture now."

Ezra rose to his feet, leaning on the canes. He towered
over Gran. "I'll head back to my room," he said. The mask
puffed in and out as he spoke.

Gran waited until Ezra made his way out of the kitchen
before she came to stand beside me.

Together we watched Ezra struggle on Gramp's canes
until he turned the corner and disappeared into his room.

 *Sixteen*

Aunt May and Uncle Lemmy owned a large dairy farm on Old Putney Road. At least it used to be a dairy farm.

Now it was nothing.

I loved this farm once, with its hundreds of black-and-white Holsteins. When you drove by, depending on the time of day, the cows would be moving across the pasture, or stopping to graze, or swishing their tails at flies. Sometimes they stood under the tin roof of the feeding sheds, or lumbered through the tunnel Aunt May and Uncle Lemmy had dug under the road. At milking time they knew to cross back toward the barns.

No trace of the cows remained. The government claimed the land around Uncle Lemmy's farm escaped fall-out, but their reports lied. Everything had the taint of contamination here—the cows, their milk, the grass they ate.

The emergency people gave Uncle Lemmy his radiation detector. He could read the levels.

"Is it safe for us to be here?" I asked as Gran pulled into the driveway.

"The rain we had last month washed most everything clean," Gran said. "Lemmy tested again though, before he let us come. The radiation is in the soil now, under the snow and ice, filtering into the groundwater. It's safe for us to visit. But not a good place for anyone to live."

We backed up to the barn nearest the house. Uncle Lemmy joined us, unloading the ewes and settling them in a clean stall. We hurried from the barn inside to Aunt May.

A hospital bed and some medical equipment took up a large portion of the living room. The rest of the room was sprawled with my cousins, all seven of them.

In the bed lay Bethany, the youngest of the girls, tubes and monitors hooked up to her. Her thin hair spread like dark wet fingers across her scalp. Bethany had taken in a high dose of radiation shortly after the accident. No one knew why she got sicker than the others. The doctors never thought she'd make it through the first month. She did.

"We're managing," Aunt May said. "But we can't sell the farm. And Lemmy here can't bring himself to leave. Not for a few months, anyway. Not until he's certain about the degree of contamination."

Twice the government had ignored high radiation levels on Aunt May and Uncle Lemmy's farm. But Uncle Lemmy couldn't ignore the readings. He wouldn't sell tainted milk, even if the government claimed it was safe.

Always in the past Aunt May and Uncle Lemmy had

laughed so easy. They had lines around their eyes and their mouths, like folding fans, from all the laughter. The lines looked uneasy on their faces now, like the creases you get from sleeping hard on a crumpled sheet. Even when my father left and my mother died, they didn't take it this hard.

It was warm for December, but Uncle Lemmy had the woodstove cranking heat. Those big cousins of mine took up the whole living room. Everywhere were slung arms, splayed legs. An odor like ripe male goats lingered beneath the bleach smell.

I'd rarely spent more than a few minutes inside this house when I visited. Usually I'd grab a sandwich or go to the bathroom. Sometimes I didn't even come in for that. We did everything outside.

"Lou? Maxine? Let's go out," I said to the two cousins closest to my age.

Both girls looked up, afraid.

"It's too hot in here," I said. "I need to get out."

My cousins wouldn't even look at me.

"Then I'll go alone." I stood.

Gran and Aunt May exchanged glances.

"How bad is it out there?" Gran asked.

"It's better," Uncle Lemmy said. "The area around the barns and the house isn't bad. And we have protective gear."

Gran looked at me. "You'll stay in the gear and only go where Uncle Lem says it's safe."

I nodded.

"Okay," Gran said.

Aunt May fussed like a broody hen as she led me to the mudroom and helped me into the layers of protective clothing. "Don't exert yourself out there, Nyle," she warned. "Don't stay out too long. And don't go beyond the pond."

I walked out the farmhouse door, taking in the familiar view, the wide, snow-covered valley. The protective boots hindered me, as did the suit. The mask, carefully set over my face by Aunt May, made breathing hard. But it was good to be out.

I walked toward the pond. I always loved that pond. I learned to swim there. Uncle Lemmy had built a floating dock, a big one, so the whole family could fit on at once. I remembered the shouts of summer, the feel of bare feet on the grass, in the pond mud, on the splintery boards of the dock.

My cousins Lou and Maxine had looked terrified when I asked them to come out with me.

I headed back toward the barns. Three long barns, identical, connected to each other by covered pathways. Red barns, the American flag painted over the door of each one. Every year, a different cousin touched up the flags with a small brush, keeping them fresh and bright.

Fog crept down the valley as I watched.

I turned toward the road, now blocked off just around the bend with concrete barriers. Two soldiers in radiation suits stood guard in shifts, never leaving the barricade unattended. Used to be a steady flow of traffic ran up and down the highway. Now, even if they could get through, no one dared. Not heading south, into the contaminated zone. Not heading north out of it. Stationing soldiers there kept looters from going in and bringing out radioactive goods to sell on the black market. The soldiers helped the occasional straggler too, stumbling out of the dead zone on foot.

Uncle Lemmy's farm sat on the very border of death. The road had died, just as the farm had died, just as Aunt May and Uncle Lemmy and my cousins were dying.

My bones ached. Maybe from the weight of the suit, maybe from the change in temperature. I looked north toward the advancing wall of fog.

Walking into the first barn, empty but for the pair of ewes we'd brought with us, I remembered how it used to be. The barns once boomed with the stomp and low of cows. Now only my footsteps echoed. And the lonely bleating of two pregnant sheep. Old smells clung to the splintery barn boards: sweet clover, baled hay, the earthy stench of cows. Ghost smells.

How much could Aunt May and Uncle Lemmy take, losing their farm, their livelihood, maybe even their children?

The government had dishonored Uncle Lemmy. Said he was trying to collect on other people's misfortunes. Trying to ride the coattails of the accident. Told him he should be ashamed with so much genuine suffering and loss. That there was nothing wrong with his farm.

But if what the government said was true, why had Uncle Lemmy destroyed a herd of prize Holsteins? Why was my cousin Bethany in a hospital bed in the living room, dying of radiation poisoning?

Knowing what had happened to his herd, to his daughter, how could Uncle Lemmy ever pasture another cow here?

Coming back into the open, the fog engulfed me. It enveloped the farm. I leaned back against the rough wall of the barn, feeling the solid boards behind me. Gramp helped build these barns. Neither he nor Gran held a grudge against Aunt May. Their argument was with my father. My argument was with him too. He started all the leaving.

In the fog the whole world disappeared.

I forgot the warning not to run, I forgot I shouldn't gulp in the air. I had to get back to the house. I needed to see Gran, rock steady in the middle of Aunt May's living room.

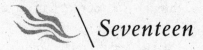 *Seventeen*

Tuesday, after dinner, Mrs. Trent led Ezra, in his mask, out of his room and down the hall to the kitchen.

"Hi, Ezra," I said.

Ezra hobbled straight past me. The trip down the hall hadn't exhausted him as it had two days earlier. He used only one of Gramp's canes this time.

"Is it still safe?" he asked.

I ran the detector in front of the windows, around the room.

Ezra didn't collapse into a chair this time. He stayed on his feet and warmed his back at the stove.

"Doing better every day," I said.

Ezra, staring right at me, removed his mask. Leaning on the cane, he limped over to the window, looked out into the blank night.

Then he turned back toward the kitchen, leaning comfortably against the sink. "Nice place," he said. "You and your grandmother have a nice place."

"Thanks. My grandfather did all the inside work. Gramp liked carpentry better than he liked sheep farming. My room upstairs, Gramp did that. I have a window seat and built-in shelves. You could come up and see if you're strong enough to climb steps."

Ezra poked his head through the door leading up to my bedroom. "I'll try."

Using the cane, he inched toward the upper landing, one slow step at a time, stopping every few moments to catch his breath. At the top he stepped aside, making room for me. I had followed behind, in case he fell. He rested on the landing, panting, leaning on the cane.

The puppy, inside for the night, followed us up the stairs. He put his paws on the quilt and barked at Bayley, asleep in the center of my mattress. Bayley shot to his feet, back arched, fur standing straight up on his spine. He hissed at the puppy and danced sideways for a step or two before streaking past us, down the stairs.

I caught the puppy before he tumbled down the steps after the cat.

Ezra got as far as my bed and sat down. The puppy put all his energy into finding an edge of my hand to gnaw on. I looked up to see Ezra eyeing my things. I wished for a collection of books like Muncie had in her room. Books had definitely been a part of Ezra's life before the accident. My nests and rocks and pinecones probably didn't interest him much.

Ezra, on the edge of my bed, struggled to catch his breath. He faced away from the window, his shoulders hunched. The window gaped like a wide toothless mouth behind him.

"Would you feel better if I brought the detector and checked things up here?" I asked.

Ezra nodded.

I put the puppy on the floor, told him to stay, and hushed by Ezra in my thick socks.

Down in the kitchen I opened the door to the woodstove. Poking coals around, I chucked another chunk of wood into the fire.

Grabbing the detector, I returned silently up the steps.

I didn't mean to spy on him, but I liked seeing Ezra in my room. As I watched from the darkened stairwell, he struggled to his feet. Ezra stopped beside the puppy who had stayed more or less where I'd told him to stay, busily sniffing my backpack.

Slowly Ezra knelt. The dog sniffed his pajamas. Their heads came closer. The puppy craned his fat neck up while Ezra brought his own face down. All at once their noses touched.

I held my breath, standing on the top step.

Then Ezra lifted the puppy into his arms and held him.

That's when I stepped into the room. "Made friends, I see."

"He's hard to resist."

Ezra put the dog down and leaned against his cane with one hand, watching me run the radiation detector around the room.

Suddenly the steady crackle of the detector changed frequency. Right in my bedroom the wand was picking up radiation.

Ezra's eyes widened. I could see the breath coming fast and shallow in his chest. Quickly I looked back to the

detector, unwilling to believe what I heard.

"What is it?" Ezra asked.

I ran the wand over my shelf again. Again the detector registered signs of radiation.

"Whatever it is, Ezra," I said, trying to reassure him, "there's only a trace."

"A trace is too much," Ezra whispered, backing toward the steps.

I forced my trembling hand to slowly scan the shelves with the wand, zeroing in on the radiation.

"It's the watches," I said at last. "Ezra. It's just my watches. Probably the paint on the dials. They're those glow-in-the-dark kind."

There were tears in Ezra's eyes.

"It's just some old broken watches, Ezra."

"Get them out of here," Ezra whispered.

"Okay. Okay," I said.

I picked up the watches, looked around for a place to hide them. "What do you want me to do with them?"

"Get them out of here. Please. Get them out."

I ran downstairs with the watches and took them into the living room, sticking them under the cushions of the couch.

Heading back to my room, I grabbed the mask from the kitchen. I found Ezra paralyzed, pale. "Would you like this back?" I asked, holding out the mask to him.

I ran the wand over everything again, carefully.

"All clear," I said.

Ezra scrubbed a hand over his eyes.

"It's all clear, Ezra."

"Where are they?"

"I put them where you won't come near them. In the living room. Under some cushions. I'll get them out of the house later."

The puppy tugged at Ezra's pant cuff. Ezra took a deep breath and let it out, shuddering.

"So, show me around, Nyle?"

Nyle. He had called me Nyle.

"Sure," I said.

I pointed out the highlights of my room. It didn't seem like much as I showed it to Ezra. He must have had a much nicer bedroom in Cookshire, a much nicer house.

Making my way over to the night table, I started reading aloud the names of the R.I.F. books I had.

"You want to borrow one?"

"Sure," Ezra said, choosing *Slake's Limbo*. "I'd really like another chance at this one. I don't remember much of it." Of course he didn't. He'd been more dead than alive while I'd read it to him.

The rest of my books featured girls as main characters or seemed too young for Ezra. I didn't see how they'd interest him. Maybe tomorrow I could borrow some books from Muncie. We were getting along better since the trip to Manchester. Maybe she'd loan me some of hers.

Ezra sat on the floor and the puppy tumbled over him. He butted Ezra with his enormous head, biting Ezra's hands with sharp puppy teeth. The dog grabbed a corner of Ezra's flannel pajama top, really one of Gramp's old shirts. He tugged at it, growling. Ezra growled back from behind the mask. The puppy let go of the shirttail in surprise. Plopping back on his bottom, he tilted his head to one side.

I laughed and sat on the floor opposite them. "Come on, dog," I called, and clapped my hands together.

The puppy bounced away from Ezra and rolled across the floor toward me.

We played with him until Mrs. Trent called Ezra down.

As he descended to the kitchen, Ezra turned once and looked over his shoulder at me. The light from my bedroom spilled down the steps to touch the mask on his face, lighting his drooping eyes, his tiny scar.

Ezra smiled.

" 'Night, Nyle," he said.

He kept staring up at me.

It felt like when the stove has been cooking all day. Every square inch of me, inside and out, felt warm. Even my toes. I watched as Ezra turned, watched the back of his curly head moving down the steps.

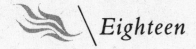 *Eighteen*

Every night Ezra climbed to my room. He came, he said, to get a new book. Muncie gladly loaned me handfuls, mostly books a boy might like. She never asked any questions. And Ezra never asked how I suddenly had so many more books than I'd had that first night.

We played with the dog each evening, Ezra and I, teaching it to fetch and stay and sit, giving it bite-sized chunks of Gran's bread as reward.

Ezra grew less dependent on Gramp's walking stick, but he carried it anyway. He tried making the puppy jump over it. Usually, though, the dog either squeezed under or tumbled around the end of the stick to get to the other side. I hid the watches in the barn and gradually Ezra gave up wearing the radiation mask again.

One day at school the principal, Mr. Perry, called me to his office during homeroom.

I walked past the empty desk where the secretary used to sit and knocked on Mr. Perry's door. Kids at school called Mr. Perry "the pencil." He was tall and thin and his skin had a yellow tint to it. Mr. Perry had stayed on through the accident, even though the town couldn't guarantee his paycheck.

He sat behind his desk, several sheets of paper spread in front of him. He ran his finger down a printed computer sheet.

"Come in, Nyle," he said. "Let's be quick so you don't miss first period."

My mouth felt dry and gummy. I tried to remember if I'd brushed my teeth that morning.

"You and your grandmother doing all right?" he asked.

"I guess."

"Your grandmother phoned last week and told me about your houseguests."

A muscle under my eye started twitching.

"It's all right, Nyle. I know you have evacuees staying with you."

I sat in the chair opposite Mr. Perry and nodded.

"I also know that you want it kept quiet," Mr. Perry said. "Particularly in the case of *these* evacuees. The families from the plant have been hardest to place." Mr. Perry leaned toward me, his thin elbows digging into the stacks of paperwork on his desk. "I've also spoken with the boy's mother. She believes he's well enough to resume his studies."

I stared at the back of Mr. Perry's computer. It needed dusting.

"These are notes from all the tenth-grade teachers," Mr. Perry explained, lifting one of the bundles of paperwork from the mess on his desk. "Here are copies of the books he'll eed. It's better this way, I think, his studying at home. To be frank, Nyle, I'm not certain most students or their families re ready for him here at Leland and Gray. You just pick up is lessons each week and he'll keep up. The staff knows bout him, and the board. But we don't have to say anything bout him to anyone else right now."

"Yes, sir."

Mr. Perry looked down at a paper on his desk. "He hould have no trouble completing the earlier assignments. He didn't miss any school until—"

I stood juggling papers and books, turning my back on Mr. Perry. I didn't want to talk about the accident.

"Anything he doesn't understand, anything unfamiliar, ust let us know."

"Yes, sir."

"Nyle," Mr. Perry said, turning to the next layer of paperwork on his desk.

I turned back toward him.

"You and your grandmother, you've done a good thing."

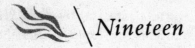 *Nineteen*

Everywhere I looked, the back bedroom showed signs of Ezra. Projects for school, maps, artwork.

The better he felt, the more he took on. He had completely monopolized the room. No outward sign of Mrs. Trent, except the neatly made cot. No trace of Gramp.

Mr. Perry was right. Ezra really hadn't missed that much school. He caught up with his class quickly.

Sometimes, sitting together doing homework, I had trouble concentrating. My eyes wandered from my notes, lingering on Ezra's legs, his eyes, his hair. He sat cross-legged on the floor, reading over his history assignment, drumming his pencil against the hard cover of his math book, against the empty cookie tins, and I could not take my eyes off him.

I had actually started believing Ezra was like everyone else, normal, healthy, a regular fifteen-year-old boy, when late one afternoon the firehouse siren went off.

The thin wail from the fire station barely penetrated the farmhouse walls, but Ezra heard the sound and froze. His knuckles went white around his pencil. The pencil snapped.

"Shut the curtain!" he cried. "Quick. Shut the curtain."

"It's just a fire, Ezra," I said. "A chimney fire somewhere. They happen a lot this time of year."

"You don't know that," Ezra insisted. "Just shut the curtain!"

I got up and did as he asked.

Ezra shrank before my eyes. He pulled himself into the corner farthest from the window, pressing his back against the striped wallpaper.

Maybe this *was* another release. The sirens kept howling, dying down, starting up again.

But then the last moan faded to silence and the silence held. Within moments a single fire truck sped past on the main road.

I felt silly with relief. It was a fire, just a fire. And terrible as that might be for the people watching their house burn, it sure beat another nuclear accident.

The afternoon remained still. If it had really been another radiation release, the sirens wouldn't have stopped. I knew that. Ezra knew it too.

"Nyle?" Ezra's voice sounded hoarse.

"Ayuh."

"Thanks."

"For what?"

Ezra stared at me. "You must think I'm a jerk."

"No," I said. "I don't."

"Well, I am a jerk," Ezra said, standing up, opening the curtain.

"If you say so."

"You're okay, Nyle, for a sheep girl."

"You got something against sheep?" I asked, crumpling a piece of notebook paper and making a basket in his trash can.

"Only that sheep follow," said Ezra. "Never lead, just follow."

"It's a good thing for sheep farmers they do." I shifted position, leaning back against Ezra's bed.

"I don't want to be a sheep anymore," Ezra said.

I stroked the puppy as it chewed the eraser on the end of my pencil. How had we gone from sheep farming to being sheep? I had trouble following his train of thought sometimes.

"The government herded us from our homes, millions of us," Ezra said. "They knew someday there would be an accident. If they hadn't believed it could happen, they wouldn't have made such elaborate plans for when it did. They knew how awful it would be too. I really think they knew. But it didn't stop them. And we just let them do it to us. Like sheep. I don't want to be a sheep anymore. I want to control my life. I want to live outside their system. Like you and your grandmother do."

"We're as dependent as anyone, Ezra. We all still have to breathe the same air."

"No," Ezra insisted. "You're not as dependent. They just have you brainwashed into believing you are."

He was wrong. Mrs. Haskins said the accident would touch us all. She knew. We had changed; the way we shopped, the way we ate, the way we worked. We changed the way we thought about things too. No more confidence in the future, no more blind trust, all because of the accident at Cookshire.

No one on this entire planet was separate from anyone else. We were all connected, by the water we drank, the air we breathed. The release of radiation from Cookshire had risen into the atmosphere. Heightened levels of radiation registered everywhere. Halfway around the world it had tainted rice crops, poisoned grazing fields, turned the air toxic where babies slept in the open.

When I dwelt on it, my stomach knotted around the things that had happened because of the accident. But good things were happening too. Right here in the back bedroom good things were happening.

Of everything in my life that had changed, that's what mattered most.

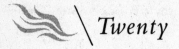 \ *Twenty*

Christmas was over. We'd tried calling Aunt May and Uncle Lemmy but we couldn't get through. The phones stayed jammed all Christmas Day.

We hadn't made a big deal of it. Gran and I never did, but especially not this year. It didn't seem right with all Mrs. Trent and Ezra had lost. Besides, Mrs. Trent didn't even celebrate Christmas.

The day after, I tromped across the fields in my heavy boots, a wool hat tugged low over my ears to keep out the sting. The puppy, growing bigger daily, rolled along beside me. Caleb pranced along at my other side.

In the bitter wind I made my rounds of the first three pastures, finishing across the main road on the flat. The day, with a windchill factor somewhere around forty below, kept my skin and eyes stinging.

The last pasture sprawled way up on the hill, the other side of the road from Muncie's house, above Ripley's place.

I could take the long way by the dirt road to get to the pasture, or I could take a shortcut through Ripley's woods. The woods, at least, offered some protection from the wind.

Cold crinkled the moisture in my eyes when I blinked. The tiny hairs inside my nose stiffened with frost. Trotting happily along beside me, the puppy and Caleb kept well insulated in their thick coats. But I couldn't stop shivering. I decided to take the shortcut.

Caleb hesitated at the foot of Ripley's land. "Smell Tyrus, eh, boy?"

Ripley's family never hauled trash. They tossed it out into the woods, leaving old cars, garbage, junked appliances rotting among the trees. They didn't care what their place looked like, what vermin the garbage drew. They didn't even care where their septic emptied.

We'd climbed about three quarters of the way to the far pasture when Ezra's puppy balked. He sat his fat rump down and wouldn't budge.

"Come on, pup," I urged. "This is no time to stop. Come on."

Just then I heard the whisper of leaves as a wiry gray shape streaked past.

The puppy jumped and barked. A squirrel raced up a bare maple tree, then edged back down, teasing.

The puppy went crazy. His yapping broke the wintry silence.

"Hush!"

But my warning came too late.

Ripley must have been outside already. Within moments he appeared, lumbering toward us, across the snow. The puppy barked enthusiastically, watching Ripley approach, but Caleb sat at my feet, growling.

"What are you doing here?" Ripley carried his rifle over his shoulder.

"Isn't hunting season over?" I asked.

As Ripley came closer, the puppy stopped wagging his tail. I didn't know where Tyrus was, but I was glad for once he wasn't here. I sure didn't want to see a dogfight. Knowing Tyrus, he probably had the wanderlust again. Maybe, as we spoke, he was running the life out of some deer.

"I was just on my way to the far pasture," I said.

"Well, keep going and don't stop till you get there."

I didn't need telling twice. I moved the dogs quickly through the woods and off Ripley's property.

Feeding the sheep and refilling their salt lick, I was surprised to see my hands shaking. The sheep butted around me as I distributed hay. I checked for limping and inspected their droppings. Everything looked fine. Ice and snow glistened on the backs of the ewes as they grazed contentedly, steamily chomping away.

Suddenly Ezra's puppy bounded toward the fence closest to Ripley's woods. His bark had a warning sound to it I hadn't heard from him before. The sheep stopped eating, scuffed together over the snow to the opposite corner of the pasture.

Ripley stood at the edge of the woods, Tyrus panting beside him.

I tried ignoring him as Muncie, bundled like a nylon ball, came rocking up the path toward us from the other direction.

"I heard barking," Muncie said.

Caleb went straight to her, his tail wagging.

If only Ezra could be here—three to one. We could take Ripley on easy with those odds.

But Ezra hid inside the house, afraid to come out.

"Hey, mutant," Ripley yelled.

"Cut it out, Ripley," I said.

"What?"

"Her name is Muncie."

"Munchie, Munchie," Ripley yelled. "She eats her own snot."

His rifle tucked under one arm, Ripley packed an ice ball and let it fly. I don't know if he was aiming for me or not, but the ice caught me on the cheek as I bent over to move the salt bucket. I went down to my knees, seeing stars.

Muncie came over and stood beside me. "Are you all right, Nyle?"

My head still swam and my cheek stung.

"Damn it, Ripley," I said.

"He's not there anymore. He ran off as soon as you went down."

Muncie examined my face. "He got you good."

"It'll be okay," I said, shrugging her off.

"Look, Nyle," Muncie said, her hand resting on Caleb's head, "thanks for sticking up for me. But you don't need to fight my battles. Ripley doesn't bother me. Only people who mean something to me can hurt me."

Muncie bent down on one knee and roughed up the puppy. Already he stood taller than her on his hind legs.

"It's about time I got to meet you," she said, nuzzling the puppy with her gloved hands. "I've seen you all over, but we haven't been properly introduced, have we, boy?" Muncie's hands were everywhere at once on Ezra's puppy. The puppy's whole body wagged with pleasure.

"When did you get him?" Muncie asked, looking up at me.

"A couple of weeks ago. He was an early present." I didn't say whose present.

"What's his name?"

"He doesn't have one yet."

Muncie looked surprised, but the puppy kept wiggling around her and she let it go.

After a while Muncie started shivering so bad, her whole body chattered.

"I have to go in," she said, wrapping her nylon arms around herself. "It's fierce out here."

I nodded, pinching my nose with the fingers of my glove as Muncie walked away.

Leading the puppy back to the front pasture, I closed him in for his second night outside. He headed straight to the warmth in the center of the flock, and the sheep tightened their circle around him.

"You look half frozen," Gran said as I tumbled with Caleb into the kitchen.

I looked out the window at the thermometer mounted on the side of the house. "Four degrees below zero. And a whole lot colder when the wind blows."

"Everything okay out there?" Gran asked, stirring dried parsley into a white sauce destined for the big pot on the stove.

"The sheep are fine," I answered.

Gran's back blocked my view of the pot. She never turned from her stirring. You couldn't leave white sauce once you started. "Nyle?" Her voice raised to little more than a whisper.

"Ayuh." I leaned toward her; the kitchen chair squeaked.

"Ezra is doing better every day," Gran said.

My heart hammered. "He's leaving, isn't he?"

"No, he's not leaving." Gran eyed me fiercely. "Not yet. The visiting nurse came. He says Ezra's ready to go outdoors."

"Anyone ask Ezra how he feels about that?"

"He needs sunlight on his skin, he needs to see nothing will hurt him out there. The nurse said it'd be okay if Ezra wanted to wear the mask."

I recalled how much Ezra had improved, just moving around the house, into the kitchen, up to my room. He *was* ready to go out.

"You're right," I said.

"Good."

"It'll give him a chance to see the puppy again."

"When's he going to name that dog?"

I shrugged. My stomach rumbled with hunger.

"The milk on the stove should be warm," Gran said. "Pour some into a mug and add a little molasses to it."

I stirred the dark, sticky syrup into a mug of milk and swilled the muzzy liquid over my tongue. Slowly, enjoying every sip, I downed the small warm comfort.

I wondered how I might persuade Ezra to come outside. Would it be enough to tell him about the way the light glistened on the sheep's icy backs today? He couldn't see that through his window.

Or I could tell him to start tending those sheep he'd been grilling me about. His interest hadn't dimmed, not after weeks of pumping me with questions.

But most likely, I just needed to tell him that's the only way he could see his puppy again.

"Gran," I said. "I'll get him out tomorrow."

"Not for too long. Remember, he's still weak."

"I can pace things."

"Okay," Gran said. "See that you do, Nyle."

Gran stirred the contents of the pot, now thickening with the addition of the white sauce.

"Do me a favor?" Gran asked. "Watch this sauce a minute, will you?" She crossed the kitchen toward the hall.

I stood by the stove, stirring the blue enamel spoon around in the pot until Gran shut the bathroom door. Then I stretched across and opened the refrigerator.

About half a pumpkin pie remained from Christmas. I pulled the plate out and broke off pieces of crust, remembering to stir the sauce every few seconds. Chewing pie shell, I used my fingers to scoop out an orange knob of pumpkin filling and popped that in my mouth too.

Smoothing all the edges, I fixed the pie, hoping Gran wouldn't notice my nibbling, and shoved the plate back inside the refrigerator before she came out. I was just swallowing the last of it when Gran entered the kitchen.

She sniffed. "You been into the pie?"

I looked down at my feet. How did she know these things?

She scanned the counter and the table—saw no fork, no plate. "With your fingers?" Gran asked.

I wiped my guilty hand on the back of my jeans.

Gran opened the old refrigerator. Cold air spilled out across the floor. "Nyle Sumner," Gran said, scowling at me. "Look what you did to this pie."

I smacked my lips, still tasting pumpkin on my tongue.

 *Twenty-one*

Gran's rear end filled the small opening to the knee-wall in my room.

"What are you after, Gran?" I asked.

Inside the knee-wall Gran mumbled.

She stored things like old lamps and paraffin and dented pots in the crawl space behind the wall.

"I can't hear you," I called.

Gran spoke up. "I'm looking for Gramp's winter things. Ezra needs warm clothes and boots if he's tramping along through chores with you this morning."

I didn't think Gran had kept Gramp's winter clothes.

"Gramp's things won't fit Ezra," I said.

"They'll fit him fine. Been fitting him all along."

I couldn't come out and say I didn't want Ezra wearing Gramp's things. I still feared the curse of that room. Maybe wearing Gramp's outdoor clothes would set the jinx back in motion. I couldn't bear it if anything happened to Ezra now.

"I've got clothes he can wear," I said.

Gran backed out of the cramped opening, a dusty, half-collapsed cardboard box in her arms. "Your clothes might fit Mrs. Trent, but they will certainly not fit Ezra."

Gran put the box down and brushed her hands off on her dress. Dust, like unmelted flakes of snow, sat on her hair. "Are you worried about taking him outside, Nyle?"

I pulled my hair back, then let it go. "I want him to get well—"

Footsteps across the kitchen. Ezra called up. "Nyle?"

"Be down in a second."

A few moments of silence, then Ezra called again. "Nyle, I was thinking—"

"I'll be down in a second!"

I came over to Gran and watched as she slid the box flap open. "I'm not as scared of taking him out as he is of going." The smell of mothballs and old wool tickled inside my nostrils. I sneezed.

Gran pulled out some yellowed newspapers, brushed away the worst of the mouse droppings, then handed the box to me. "Let him choose what he wants out of here. Tell him to shake things out good before he wears them."

I carried the box down the steps to the kitchen, where I found Ezra with his back to the outside door, fists clenched. When he saw me, he reached for the mask on his face.

"Nyle, I—"

I interrupted. "Gran thought you might find some warm clothes in this box. Go through and pull out what you can use. It's not as cold as yesterday, but you'll be glad of this stuff."

I tugged my coat on. Ezra watched me, started to say

something, then gritted his teeth. Pulling things out of the musty, water-stained box, he scrambled to match me, hat for hat, glove for glove.

"See you later, Gran," I called up the steps to my room. "Come on, Ezra. Come on, Caleb. Let's see how the puppy did last night."

Mrs. Trent stood in the hallway, blocking Ezra's escape to the back bedroom. She made a gesture for Ezra to pull his hat down over his ears. Ezra glared at her.

I pushed the kitchen door open and stepped outside. I expected Ezra to hesitate, but he followed right behind. He gasped as the cold air hit him, his mask collapsing in.

Okay, Ezra was out the door. I hoped the cold weather would keep Ripley and Muncie in, so I wouldn't have to explain anything. The skin on my face tightened with cold.

"Do you have the detector?" Ezra asked, looking nervous. I handed it to him. "You take it," I said, "but everything is safe, Ezra, I promise. It's all safe here. You can go without the mask if you want."

The puppy barked once from the front pasture, pacing back and forth, his tail wagging. He didn't mind the cold at all.

Ezra walked, sweeping the radiation detector in front and to the side, ready to bolt back toward the farmhouse any second. His rapid breathing made the gauze mask flutter in and out. But the radiation detector ticked harmlessly.

"Let's go, Ezra," I said. "We've got sheep to tend."

Ezra walked close enough that our coats brushed sometimes, close enough that he tripped me once by catching the back of my boot with his foot. "Sorry," he mumbled through the mask.

He struggled to keep pace with me in the icy air. I slowed down, the way I did with Muncie. Ezra hadn't been outside in a long time.

We headed for the front pasture first, to let the puppy out. As soon as I opened a wedge in the portable fence, the knee-high dog barked with excitement and bounded over to Ezra. He tumbled like a small white mountain around his feet, making sweet squeals of pleasure.

It was a good ache, watching their reunion, Ezra and the puppy. That dog had gotten Ezra outside after all.

The sheep stood in the snow, packed together like a giant ball of wool.

"These are ewes," I said.

"You's?" Ezra asked. "Like you's and me's?"

I bit the inside of my cheek. "Ewes are female sheep. Remember?"

Ezra's eyes teased. He stared at the sturdy barrels of wool. Breathed a little deeper. "They smell kind of warm and greasy," he said.

"That's the lanolin in their wool."

"Are they cold?"

"Would you be if you were wearing a coat like that?"

"A little, maybe," Ezra said.

"Exactly how they feel."

"I used to wonder," Ezra said, "what it would be like, living outside all the time. That was before—" Ezra shivered and drew his shoulders in toward his chest. The mask fluttered.

"These girls are hungry, Ezra," I said gently.

"So feed them." He sounded tired and cranky. "Aren't they your responsibility?"

"We're out of hay. We have to go back to the barn and fill the pickup."

Ezra's eyes lit up. "We drive the truck?"

I took his hand and pulled him back toward the house and the barn and Gran's beat-up old Ford, parked inside the tractor shed.

Ezra walked with wonder around the pieces of farm equipment sitting in the bays. "You never told me about this stuff."

It had been right outside his window.

"You never asked."

"Oh, man," Ezra said, putting down the radiation detector to run his gloved hands over the shiny metal fenders of the tractors. He stroked the hard black seats.

"You know how to drive?" I asked.

Ezra's eyes danced. "You mean drive one of these?"

"You can drive the truck for starters. As long as you promise not to run it into a ditch. I'll get the hay loaded."

I backed the truck inside the barn and untied the rope holding the rusty tailgate.

Ezra started toward the nearest stack of hay.

"Not that," I called. "That's first cutting." I pointed to the greenish mountain of hay bales toward the back of the barn. "We'll use second cutting today."

Ezra tried helping with the hay. The mask slipped down around his neck. He didn't notice. He seemed to have forgotten about radiation for the moment. Even though he hardly had the strength, he struggled, working beside me. Ezra moved one bale to my four.

With the truck loaded, he squatted, trying to catch his

breath. He nuzzled the puppy's huge head. "Can he ride in the truck with us?"

"No, he can *not* ride in the truck with us. The back is full of hay and he's too big to sit in the cab. He'll follow along behind, with Caleb. Got it?"

"Got it," Ezra agreed.

"Okay," I said. "You want me to drive her first so you can see how it's done?"

Ezra hesitated. He wanted behind that wheel in the worst way.

"Climb in," I ordered.

I adjusted the throttle on the old pickup. Pushed in the clutch and the brake, and turned the key. The truck snorted once and died. Pulling out the throttle a little farther, I tried again. This time when the truck snorted, I gave it a little more gas and it roared to life. I flashed Ezra the thumbs-up sign. He returned the gesture. The puppy backed away, barking. But Caleb trotted calmly ahead. He knew the routine.

"Okay," I called over the noisy truck. I pointed down in the direction of the front pasture. "We start over there."

Ezra sat on the passenger's side, exhausted, clearly relieved to be sitting down. For a moment I caught a glimpse of the boy in Gramp's bed, lost between life and death. I saw a ghost, leaning his head back against the truck cab. Then the ghost was gone.

Ezra never took his eyes off my hands and feet, watching as I went from first to second. I stopped the pickup outside the front pasture and began unloading hay. Ezra stood in front of the truck and watched, already too weak to help move another bale.

I motioned him into the pasture to join me.

He stepped back, a look of alarm crossing his face. He was afraid to get in with the sheep.

"They won't bite, you know."

With a little coaxing, Ezra finally came in. The sheep scattered away, shuffling toward the opposite fence.

The puppy stayed beside him, staring adoringly at Ezra. He wagged his tail over the white glazed snow.

When I'd distributed hay, filled the salt feeder, and satisfied myself that all was well in the pasture, I turned back to the truck.

"Well, Ezra. Time for the next delivery. Ready to drive?"

He pointed to himself. "Now?"

"Ayuh."

Ezra climbed into the driver's seat. I showed him what each pedal and knob was for.

"Push the clutch in, press down the brake, and turn her on," I said. "When you've got her running, let up on the brake, let out the clutch, and give her some gas. If she feels like stalling, push in the clutch till she evens out. Got it?"

Ezra took a moment more to study the knobs and pedals. Then he pushed in the clutch and turned the key. The engine caught on the first try and held. Ezra grinned wide enough to unhinge his jaw.

I let the puppy out of the pasture and led the way on foot, making the rounds of the farm. Ezra followed slowly behind me in the truck, not too smooth on the pedal, but good enough. Hardly stalled out more than four, five times.

We fed the sheep in all four pastures. Ezra, who hadn't been off his deathbed a month yet, looked exhausted but happy in a way I'd never seen before.

At the end of the morning he drove the truck back to the shed and parked it.

The puppy leaned against him and Ezra ruffled the thick white fur.

"When are you going to name that dog?" I asked.

Ezra stooped and the puppy bathed him in kisses, knocking off his hat in the process.

"I've been thinking about it," Ezra said.

"So?"

"What do you think about—Shep?"

His first name for me.

I nodded. "Perfect."

"Shep!" Ezra tried out the name. "Here, Shep!"

The dog turned to Ezra and bounded over.

Ezra laughed. "Look, Nyle. He knows his name."

"You could have called him anything, Ezra. You could have called him sheep-dip and he'd have come."

Ezra ran his hand over the thick fur. He buried his face in Shep's side. "Good dog," he said. "Good Shep."

"Hey, I'm starving," I said, looking at the circles under Ezra's eyes and the way his hands shook.

Ezra nodded. "I'm hungry too."

"First we have to put your brilliant dog in the front pasture. Come on, Shep. Come on, boy."

After we'd closed the puppy inside the fence, I started up the hill toward home. Ezra put his hand out and stopped me.

"Wait," he said. "Could we wait just a minute?"

He stood in the middle of the road. Within his sight for the first time, stone fences snaked the borders of old pastures, woods of birch and maple cast shadows across the snow. Distant mountains humped their rounded backs against the cold. Ezra sighed. "I used to hike to a place like this. With a couple friends of mine. I'll never see that place again. I'll never see my friends again."

I turned to Ezra, touched the arm of Gramp's coat sleeve, then lowered my hand. Ezra shivered beside me.

He wrapped his arms around himself and squinted into the cold sun. The wind whipped his brown curls around the edges of his hat. I couldn't even see the scar with his hat and his hair like that. My breath caught, looking at him. What it did inside me to look at him.

"Everyone died that day," Ezra said, quietly.

"No they didn't," I said. "You didn't."

"I did," Ezra said.

"Then who drove the pickup truck this morning?"

"Remember," he said. "I'm the phoenix, rising out of my own ashes."

I nodded.

"I never saw someone die before," Ezra said.

For a moment I saw the sheet over my mother's face, I saw Gramp's coffin lowered into the ground. I heard his tired bones knock against the plain pine box he'd built himself.

"I know how it feels to watch someone die," I said.

But did I understand what Ezra was feeling?

"Why am I still here?" Ezra asked. "When hundreds of others are dead, why am I still here?"

"Ezra—"

"My father managed the plant. Did you know that? We owed everything we had to Cookshire. We had a great life, Nyle. Lots of money, lots of things." Ezra's laugh rasped with sarcasm. "Where are all those things now?"

I looked out over the hills. A hawk circled high overhead.

Something in the woods was dying. The hawk bided its time, making large, easy circles, waiting.

"I hated my father's job at the plant. We fought about it. My father said, 'It's a job, Ezra. How else am I supposed to support you and your mother?' But it was more than a job to him. He believed in what he was doing. He believed he could control it. That he could control the people who controlled it. He really believed nothing would ever happen."

I looked down at the trampled snow. I didn't know what to say, what to do.

Ezra's teeth chattered. "I told my father, if anything ever went wrong, if there was ever an accident, it would be his fault. For accepting nuclear money, for accepting nuclear risk. It would be his fault. I never really thought—"

Ezra's chin trembled and he put his hand up to hide it. "I told him, if anything ever went wrong, he'd burn in hell because of it."

Ezra was silent a moment.

"The night of the accident, my father—he helped so many people—got them out of the plant. He kept going in, soaking up more radiation.

"Even after he couldn't stand up straight, stumbling, throwing up, he wanted to go back. If I hadn't said those things to him—Nyle, if I hadn't said—he might have walked away. Some guys on duty that night—they walked away. Ran away. My father might still be alive."

Staring across at the snow-covered hills, I made myself keep breathing and just listened.

"I sat by his bed—watched him. I needed to talk to him, needed to say—" Ezra's arms crossed over his chest. "His skin so awful—scabbed and bubbled—like leather. He said nothing. I waited. Then one day he spoke. Not to me, to Mother. 'Miriam,' he said. 'Miriam.' And then he died."

I took a deep breath. The cold ached in my throat.

"Did you ever think he kept going back inside the plant because he felt responsible for the people in there?" I asked.

Ezra looked across the field and shrugged.

"Ezra, what he did at the plant that night might have had nothing to do with you."

Ezra rubbed his eyes with his hand. "The fact is, Nyle, no matter what, I can't take back what I said. I'd always put the blame on him, but I wore the clothes nuclear money paid for, I ate the food. I lived in the house."

"Ezra—"

"When I was so sick with radiation, I thought I saw my father. I tried catching up to him. He stood right in front of me. I put my hand on his shoulder. His skin came away in my fingers."

"No, Ezra."

I took Ezra's wrists in my hands and stared into his face. Then slowly, slowly, I wrapped my arms around him. He lowered his head onto my shoulder. I took off my glove and touched him. My fingers whispered over Gramp's coat, over Ezra's back.

"The hardest part is letting go," I said.

Ezra was weeping. Maybe for the first time, weeping.

"You *are* like the phoenix, Ezra," I said. "You have to rise up out of all this mess and start again." I didn't want him to leave, but I understood now that he had to. "Fly away, Ezra," I said. "Fly away and start again."

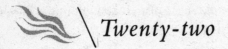 *Twenty-two*

Ezra and I headed toward the farm-house. He kept his eyes lowered, but he reached over and held my hand.

I felt connected to Ezra in some way I hadn't let myself feel in a long time, and though I liked it, really liked it, deep inside I sensed its danger.

When Ezra came to us, it forced me to live with the accident after most people had managed to go on. Night and day, I worried about him dying in that room. I tried keeping it my life, just my life. But there was more to all of this than just me. All around me was Ezra, and because of him, all the others like Ezra.

It only took a moment and so many lives had changed forever. Ezra felt guilty because he'd lived on nuclear money. But how about the rest of us? Weren't we just as guilty?

I had been out late that night with the sheep. The grass, clean and thick; the pasture, patterned with moon shadows.

All the chores long done, and just like that, everything had changed. And I didn't even know it.

If people really understood how big this was, how far it went, how deep, something would be done. Now. To change things. So this could never happen again.

But unless people lived what Ezra'd lived, unless they'd seen what Ezra had seen, how could they understand? How could anyone understand? Ezra's father hadn't understood and he knew more about the dark side of nuclear power than most of us.

And the people who understood now, the people who had lived through it, what voice did they have? They hid in shock inside evacuation centers, inside hospitals, inside houses like ours, battling radiation sickness. They'd lost their homes, their money, their power. Who would speak for them?

A plume of smoke hung over the house. I inhaled and sighed. Ezra looked up at the sky, alarmed.

"Don't worry," I said. "It's just Gran burning green wood."

Ezra's hand felt large and comfortable around mine. Between us a connection, a belonging. I turned to him.

For a second I saw Gramp there, in the old coat. I caught my breath. But no, this wasn't Gramp.

This was Ezra Trent, and he was alive. The pressure of his body, warm and solid, next to mine. The clean smell of his hair.

"I need to grab an armload of wood," I said.

"Can I help?"

I eyed him in his odd assortment of outdoor clothes. His nose and his cheeks ruddy with cold, the mask hanging down around his chin, his shoulders rounded with exhaustion.

"You think you can handle it?"

Ezra made a face. "Sure I can."

He started gathering logs in his arms.

"Hey. You only need to bring a few."

He ignored me.

Boys!

While he struggled, I lifted the log carrier off the hook, filling it up so I had nearly twice the load Ezra had.

"That's cheating," Ezra said.

Both of us staggered under the weight of our loads. The bulging carrier bumped painfully against my shins as I lugged it across the yard from the woodshed.

When I turned to open the kitchen door, I caught a glimpse of someone out of the corner of my eye. Muncie. She stood at the end of our driveway. Maybe she'd seen Ezra and me outside and had come to investigate.

I turned away, acting as if I hadn't seen her at all. I had too much to think about. Ezra had been through so much already today. What if Muncie said something? I didn't want to tangle with her. We hadn't made eye contact. I thought it would be all right.

But it wasn't.

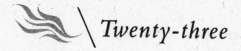 Twenty-three

Flying down the road, I barely caught the bus the next morning.

Muncie spread her backpack across the entire seat, making it clear I wouldn't be joining her.

I moved to the back.

Rudie Barrie, a seventh grader, climbed on and Muncie made room for her. Muncie and Rudie kept a steady conversation going the whole way to school.

Leave it alone, I thought, leave it alone. But I couldn't leave it.

"Hi," I said, sliding into the seat behind them. The bus bumped over the frost-heaved road.

"Hi, Nyle," Rudie said, glancing back. Usually eighth graders had nothing to do with kids from seventh.

Muncie didn't turn around. I could feel the stiff line of her shoulders.

"Supposed to be a big storm coming this afternoon. Maybe they'll call school tomorrow," I said.

"Wouldn't break my heart," said Rudie.

"Mine either," I said.

"Who cares," Muncie said. "Who cares about *your* heart?"

"Maybe no one," I said softly.

"Then quit breathing down my neck," Muncie said. "I mean it."

"I only wanted to say hello."

"Well, you said it."

Muncie rounded her shoulders like a short blue wall. Rudie looked uncomfortable. She got up and moved a couple seats away.

I leaned forward, smelling the metal rail along the top of the bus seat.

Muncie drew tighter into herself.

"Muncie, listen," I said.

"I'm a captive audience, aren't I?"

"His name is Ezra, Ezra Trent. He's one of the evacuees. He and his mother had nowhere to go after the accident. Gran asked them to stay with us. He was sick. Really sick. His father died from the radiation. The thing is, Munce, I wanted to help. He's just a regular kid. I wished so many times you could meet him and see for yourself. See that he wasn't a mutant or anything."

I slid my lip under my upper teeth and sighed. "Muncie, you're my best friend. And I don't want to lose you. But I like spending time with him, too. He's not a freak, and he's not going to make anybody sick."

The bus ground up the last hill, pulled in at the circular driveway in front of school, and chattered to a stop.

Muncie gathered her things; I followed her off the bus, followed her out of the line.

"Nyle Sumner. How can you say you're my best friend? /147 You had him at your house all this time. You never said anything."

"I couldn't. You were afraid of him."

Kids filed past, glancing over, curious.

"I thought you were different from other people. I thought you knew me, understood me. If you knew me, really knew me, you wouldn't have kept him a secret."

"But I asked how you felt about people like Ezra. You said they were freaks. They terrified you, Muncie. How could I tell you?"

"You should have been honest. You should have left it up to me."

Most of the kids had cleared the bus and entered school.

"If you'd explained—" she said.

"I tried."

"You didn't try hard enough. How could you believe I would turn away from someone with problems? Me. The biggest freak of all. How could you believe I would judge him?"

"I'm sorry," I said. "But your parents—"

"Forget about them. This is between you and me. You found time for everything else. For the sheep, and school. You found time for a complete stranger. I had to force you to spend time with me. I was good enough before he came along, but now you've got someone you like better. Someone who's less of a freak than I am. You chose him over me. You shut me out. Just like everyone else does, you shut me out."

"I didn't, Muncie."

But she was right. I had. I had treated Muncie the way all the kids at school treated her. I'd treated her like she had no feelings, no understanding. I'd treated her like she wasn't even there.

The bell rang and still we stood outside.

"Muncie, I'm sorry. I was so stupid."

"You're telling me? Just because you know sheep doesn't mean you know anything. I trusted you, Nyle. I talked to you. I thought, Nyle accepts me. Really accepts me. But you never did. You couldn't have."

I saw the pain in her eyes, like something alive. Tears flowed angrily down into her mask.

"From now on just leave me alone. Okay? Don't do me any favors. Don't pretend to like me. Don't pretend you're my friend."

Mr. Bashaw rushed past us on his way in to school.

"What are you two doing out here? Get inside! You'll both need late slips!"

Muncie turned her back on me and hitched herself into school.

Now I remembered the worst part. The worst part of making connections to people was when those connections broke.

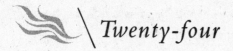 *Twenty-four*

School passed in a blur; only Ezra remained in focus.

He awaited my return each afternoon. We studied together. Sometimes he read aloud. Being with Ezra was so comfortable, so easy.

Mrs. Trent and Ezra joined us for dinner every night now. In fact, they *cooked* dinner most times. No more one-pot stews. Mrs. Trent was even starting to look less gaunt.

And the two of them, Ezra and Mrs. Trent, they cleaned our house. Really cleaned it. The cobwebs across the ceiling beams disappeared. They washed curtains, scoured rust spots. They even scrubbed the awful wallpaper in the back bedroom. The house settled into a new look.

And at night, after Ezra and I went to bed, Mrs. Trent and Gran leaned across the kitchen table. Talking, laughing.

Hearing Gran laugh softened the last calluses around my heart.

・ ・ ・

One afternoon, working on an art project, I sang softly under
my breath.

Ezra looked up. "I've heard that song before."

I stopped.

"No, don't stop. What is that?"

" 'Tender Shepherd.' I learned it for chorus."

"You sang it to me. When I was sick. I remember."

"You couldn't remember."

"But I do."

I looked down at my book, embarrassed.

At dinner Ezra told about remembering the song.

That's how we got on the subject of music.

Mrs. Trent liked music. Classical especially. Between
Gran's country and my rock, we must have driven her crazy.
Shortly after she came, she asked if we had an extra radio. She
listened to it in the living room, tuned to a public station that
drifted in and out of range. Sometimes she played our old
piano, too. The cold would stop her after a while, that and
the piano being so out of tune.

"You like jazz?" Gran asked, spooning a second helping
of scalloped potatoes onto her plate.

Mrs. Trent nodded.

"There's a concert at the school tonight," Gran said.
"Nyle brought home an announcement. I found it in the
trash."

Ezra made a face at me.

"Gran, you hate school concerts. And half the jazz band
moved away. It won't be any good."

"Maybe Ezra and Mrs. Trent would like to go," Gran
said.

Mrs. Trent touched the corner of her mouth with a napkin. "Actually, I would love to go," she said in her soft accent. "I sang when I was a girl." For a moment her eyes rested on her ugly skirt, her roughened hands. She lifted her hair from her neck with her long fingers and swung her head back and forth. "It would be nice to get out."

"But—" I said. What if people found out who they were?

"It'll be good for everyone," Gran said.

Gran had made up her mind.

We crowded onto the bench seat of the rusty pickup, squeezed so tight we could barely breathe. Gran banged my leg every time she shifted gears. We arrived late for the concert. We couldn't find four seats together. Ezra and I stood in back, leaning against the cinder-block wall of the gym. I hoped no one would notice us.

It surprised me how many people came. The gym wasn't packed like it used to be for a concert, but the cushioned seats were filled. Maybe, like Mrs. Trent, other people needed to get out, to forget about things for a while, to just enjoy a little music. Leland and Gray always gave great concerts.

Mrs. Trent boogied in her seat. I stared. This was a different side of her. How could I live with her every day and know so little about her?

Gran looked miserable. Little brown tone-deaf gnome. She rugged around in her seat, looking up at the naked ceiling. People came over to say hello during intermission. She introduced Mrs. Trent to them. No one knew who Mrs. Trent was, who she really was. No one suspected. Gran just said, "Meet my friend, Miriam." She made it so simple.

After the concert, we crossed the street to the lunch counter at Townshend General Store and ordered french fries to go.

It was almost nine, and they were closing. We couldn't sit at a table to eat. "How are we going to eat in the truck?" I asked. "I can't even move my arms."

Ezra shifted and flipped a fry into the air in the crowded truck cab, catching it in his mouth.

I tried it too.

Ezra rarely missed, but my fries ended up all over the truck, behind the bench seat, in Mrs. Trent's hair. One dropped into Gran's lap.

Ezra and I couldn't stop laughing. We got Gran and Mrs. Trent laughing too.

It hurt, laughing that hard, all squeezed together, but we couldn't stop. It's a wonder Gran didn't have an accident.

When I ran out of french fries, I grabbed Mrs. Trent's nearly full package—like she was family or something.

"Nyle," Gran snapped.

I felt a zap, like the electric fence.

"I'm sorry." I handed the fries back to Mrs. Trent.

"Take them," Mrs. Trent said. "I am having more fun watching you eat them anyway."

But I wouldn't take them back. Ezra took them instead. Before long he had us all laughing again.

The next week, Gran drove Mrs. Trent and Ezra into Montpelier for an appointment with some state people. They hoped to figure out how Mrs. Trent could get hold of some money.

"Nyle, you stay here and go to school," Gran said. "After

last week, there's no question about all of us going. The truck can't take it. Anyway, someone has to stay behind and mind things."

The old knot tightened. What if Gran came home alone? What if Ezra and his mother found a better place to stay? What if they moved thousands of miles away, to the west coast, or back to Israel with Mrs. Trent's family? She'd had another letter from them.

After school, I entered the empty house, did the chores, fixed a snack. I tried working on an essay for history. I couldn't concentrate. In my closet hung several dresses. I never wore dresses. I remembered Mrs. Trent in her seedy outfit at the concert, I remembered Gran saying my clothes wouldn't fit Ezra but they would fit Mrs. Trent.

Taking the dresses off their hangers, I folded them into a neat pile. I pulled clothes from my drawers, too.

Padding downstairs, I placed the clothing for Mrs. Trent on the kitchen table and searched for Bayley, or Caleb, any living thing would do. But the animals had curled up together by the stove. It would have been cruel to move them. Outside, Shep sat alert in the back pasture. At four months he was almost as big as the yearling sheep.

I stoked the fire and carried the pile of clothes down the hall to Ezra's room.

Light spilled through the open doorway. The room was bright now, the curtain pulled wide open. Yellow shafts of sun slanted in, dappling the floor, warming the bed.

I opened the top drawer in the dresser and found the scraps of things Mrs. Trent had collected since coming to stay with us. There were her letters, in blue airmail envelopes, two stamps fixed in each corner.

One by one I put the clothes from my closet and my drawers into Mrs. Trent's dresser.

I stood before Ezra's bed, touched my hand to his quilt, remembered Shep peeing there.

Brushing back the sides of my hair, I sighed and sat down on the bed's edge. In every corner the room reflected Ezra. I saw him immersed in a book. Bounding after the puppy. Cross-legged on the floor. Banging on the Christmas tins.

I lay down, carefully fitting my body to the peaks and valleys Ezra had left in the mattress. I turned softly, buried my face in his pillow. I could smell Ezra's hair.

One of his curls clung to the pillow case. I picked it up between my thumb and my finger, played it over my cheeks, over my lips, down my neck. Closing my eyes, I imagined Ezra, beside me, up on his elbow, talking, tucking my hair behind my ear. I imagined touching his face, certain of the way it would feel under my fingertips. In my mind I traced the crags around his eyes, touched the cresent scar.

I stayed there a long time, filling myself with Ezra.

Gran, Mrs. Trent, and Ezra arrived home shortly after dinner, looking tired.

"Well?" I asked, panting. I'd been in the back pasture when they pulled in.

"Mostly a runaround," Gran said.

Mrs. Trent added. "They know where we are. They will be in touch. We reached no decision. I hope you can extend your hospitality a little longer."

Extend our hospitality? I never wanted Ezra to leave. I didn't want Mrs. Trent leaving either.

"We did decide one thing," Ezra said. "We decided it was

time I went back to school. To Leland and Gray, Nyle! With you."

"That's terrific," I said, but I didn't feel that terrific about it. "Are you sure you're well enough? Did you see a doctor or anything?"

How was I going to explain him? Could I act as smooth as Gran had at the concert? How would it change things between us when he wasn't so dependent on me anymore?

Ezra grinned. "I'm fine. Great. The question is, is that school big enough for the two of us?"

"I doubt it," I said.

Mrs. Trent turned and placed her hand over mine. "Ezra's recovery would not be possible without you, Nyle."

I shook my head. "I didn't do anything."

Mrs. Trent continued, sandwiching my hand between her long fingers. "There are many things in this life that people do alone. But not this. This you helped Ezra to do, Nyle. And I thank you." And then she took my face between her hands and she kissed me softly on the forehead.

Twenty-five

   The bus pulled up before Ezra and I got down to the road. Fortunately, it always took Muncie time to climb on. The driver waited for her to sit. That gave us time to run the last few yards across the bridge and up the bus steps.

  Muncie busied herself as we came past her. Ezra and I sat all the way in back. The couple kids already in their seats showed a sleepy interest in Ezra, nothing more. One girl, a senior, looked Ezra over, then nodded to me.

  "She thinks we're going together," I whispered in his ear.

  Ezra's arm pressed against my shoulder as we sat, huddled together in the backseat. "Aren't we?"

  "No."

  "Oh."

  "Did you think we were going together?" I asked.

  "We're here, we're together, we're going—" Ezra shrugged.

  I couldn't tell if he was teasing.

We went straight to the office and checked Ezra in officially. Ezra gave Mr. Vernon, the new secretary, his paperwork from Montpelier and a note from the visiting nurse.

More kids were staring now.

I guided Ezra to his homeroom. The last I saw of him, he sat loose and easy in his seat. The girls couldn't keep their eyes off him.

Occasionally I caught sight of him during the day, moving from class to class. He always had two or three girls around him. I heard one ask him where he came from. Ezra said, "Down south." The girl didn't ask where down south. She accepted "Down south" as good enough.

Ezra sprawled his long legs out into the bus aisle on the ride home. He rehashed his day. "My math teacher practically had a coronary when I answered the problem of the week. She posts a brain teaser every Monday on the top left-hand corner of the blackboard. Apparently no one ever solves them."

Ezra could describe the people he'd met so well, I knew who he was talking about even when he couldn't remember their names.

Once, Muncie turned in our direction. Then Rudie started talking to her and slowly Muncie turned away again.

I guess I heaved a pretty big sigh. Ezra looked from me to Muncie, then back to me again. But he didn't say a word.

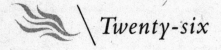

Twenty-six

Every afternoon that week, Ezra offered to help with chores. But he looked so tired at the end of the day, I told him I didn't need him. At any rate, after dinner each night we'd park ourselves at the kitchen table to tackle homework.

Ezra usually finished before me. It all came so easy to him. I'd be procrastinating, putting off something I didn't want to do, while he'd whip through math, English, science.

"Mrs. Haskins wants us to write a letter to the person in history who's had the greatest impact on us," I told Ezra.

"Tough one," Ezra said.

We'd just finished a unit on World War II, so I started thinking along those lines. I considered the people I'd read about who had survived concentration camps. And the ones who hadn't survived.

As I sorted through my ideas, Ezra pulled a fresh sheet of

paper out of his notebook, uncapped his pen, and began writing.

"What are you doing?" I asked.

"Thought I'd do the assignment with you. Keep you company," said Ezra.

"You don't have to."

Ezra shrugged and kept writing.

As I stared at my blank notebook, Ezra filled one side of a page. His script slanted every which way.

"You have lousy penmanship," I said, trying to read his sentences upside down.

"You're one to talk," Ezra answered, moving his arm so I couldn't see his paper.

At last I started writing too.

I read over my words, changing one here, crossing out a phrase there.

Finally Ezra put his pen down and looked up.

"Can I read mine to you?" I asked. "I picked Anne Frank."

Ezra nodded.

"Dear Anne Frank:

"You are the person from history who had the greatest impact on my life. Though you never reached adulthood, you taught me more than many people twice your age. Your death opened my eyes to the horror of prejudice and war."

I looked at Ezra. His chin rested on his fist as he leaned on the kitchen table.

"I admire your courage and your, and your—" I had trouble deciphering my own scribble. *"—and your—spirit."*

Caleb paced over, his nails clicking on the linoleum, and rested his head in Ezra's lap.

"You and your family had to live in fear, every waking and sleeping moment. There was never any break for you. But you kept on. You helped each other. Sometimes you got on each other's nerves. I can understand that."

I thought about Gran. I thought about Ezra and his mother.

"You were an ordinary girl forced into an extraordinary situation. Your death keeps all of us from forgetting what you died for."

I took a deep breath. "Well? What do you think?"

Ezra stared into space and I wondered if he'd heard one word.

"It's good, Nyle," he said at last, as if waking from a dream. His eyes blinked against the light, even though the light had been on the whole time. "It's good."

Ezra looked so strange, as if something hurt inside him. Suddenly he stood. Crumpling his paper, he tossed it into the trash.

"Ezra." I don't know why my heart rapped so hard against my ribs, but I wished it would stop. Had what I written upset him? I didn't mean to upset him. "Ezra, what I said about Anne Frank, I feel about you, too. What I said about courage and spirit. I think you have every bit as much as she had."

"Do I have to die in the end too so people won't forget what I died for?"

"No!" I cried.

"I'm tired, Nyle." Ezra walked away from me. He didn't say good night.

"Wait! Ezra?" I raced after him, stopping in the doorway of the kitchen.

Ezra looked up.

"I'm sorry I wrote something that hurt you."

"It's okay."

"Good night, Ezra."

"Good night."

My mouth felt dry. I sat back down in the kitchen to wait. When I was certain he wouldn't come out again for the night, I went over to the trash can, reached in, and pulled out the crushed paper.

Sitting on my window seat, I gathered Bayley into my lap. Carefully I uncrumpled and smoothed Ezra's letter.

Dear Nyle,

The first time I remember seeing you, you came with your hair full of wind and sunlight, smelling of autumn and sheep. You didn't want me here, though you never told me so. You say a lot without talking. That's the way in your house. You learned it from your grandmother.

You guided me back to health the way you guide your sheep, patiently, gently, in single syllables. You made room for me.

When I was sick, you took care of me. You fed me, you sang to me when you thought I couldn't hear. I was a stranger, a threat, yet you did these things for me.

I stared at my rough hands holding the paper he had held. I swallowed hard.

You look happiest when you're outside, with your sheep. You taught me to drive a truck. You taught me to let in the sunlight, to let myself breathe again. You taught me to let go of the things I couldn't change. You forgave me and accepted me without judging me. You have given me a reason to keep going. There can be no greater impact on a life than that. I thank you, Nyle. I thank you with all my heart.

Forever,
Ezra

I read the letter again, and then again. And then once more. I read it until it had become part of me, something I could carry with me always.

Forever Ezra.

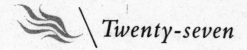 *Twenty-seven*

       The second week after Ezra started school, we had an early thaw. Snow began melting, leaving pockets around the trunks of trees. The dirt road that led to our house turned to mud each afternoon and froze in deep ruts each evening. Outside, during the day, a steady dripping signaled the thawing of snow banks. Inside, the sun warmed our house.

Ezra and I got off the bus one afternoon, heading home. Halfway up the muddy road, Muncie trailing behind us in her slow shuffle, we saw Ripley Powers emerge from the woods. Ripley had kept his distance from Ezra. He hadn't really been in school that much lately.

    "What'd you do, Nyle? Trade one mutant for another?"

    I looked first at Ezra walking beside me, then back over my shoulder at Muncie, struggling alone up the lane.

"Ignore him," I whispered to Ezra, but I slowed my pace, unwilling to leave Muncie behind unprotected.

"He's a mutant!" Ripley glared at Ezra through his good eye, his bad one narrowed down to a slit. "You think I'm dumb, but I know an evacuee when I see one. All uppity looking. He's one of them Boston types. Bet I know what you're doing with him too. Making yourself some mutant babies, aren't you?"

I saw black, suddenly black, everywhere around me.

"Enough!" I yelled.

I threw down my backpack and lunged at Ripley Powers.

Fury screamed like a dark and blinding steam inside me. My hands burned as they struck again and again against his hard bones.

Ripley towered over me. He extended his arm, holding me just out of reach. Staring down at me, he laughed.

That's when I saw Ezra coming for him.

Ripley was built like a shell casing, hard and tapered and cold.

I remembered once thinking if Ezra and Muncie and I went up against Ripley, we could beat him. Now I saw the truth of it. Ezra wasn't a fighter.

Even if Muncie joined in, we didn't stand a prayer against Ripley Powers.

With Ezra's approach, Ripley shoved me out of the way.

Seemed like he'd been waiting for Ezra all his life.

Ripley took Ezra down easy, with one punch. He pushed Ezra, face first, into the mud. Ezra never got one good shot. Ripley flipped him over.

"Stop," I screamed. "Ripley, stop it."

Ripley had a rhythm to his violence. He hit Ezra over and over. Ezra started to bleed.

I tore up behind Ripley and pulled at him, trying to haul /165 him off Ezra. His hair was too short to grab hold. He wrenched my fingers from his coat with a snap of his shoulders.

"Leave him alone, Ripley," I screamed.

Blood gushed from Ezra's nose.

I pummeled Ripley's head and neck and back with my fists. He pushed me aside hard, into the pricker bushes along the bank.

Ezra was bleeding more now, from his mouth, from his ears.

"Look what you're doing to him, Ripley," I cried. "You're killing him. Stop it! Stop it!"

But Ripley would not stop.

"He's one of those mutants, isn't he? I knew you had him there in your house. Living with you. Sleeping with you. I knew it all along. Well, we don't need no more mutants in this world," Ripley said. He hit Ezra again, and again.

I screamed, throwing myself at him. I scratched at his ears, his face, his eyes. I must have caught his bad eye. He howled with pain and sprang off Ezra, grabbing me by the wrist.

Ripley pulled me down into the mud, pinning my arms. The look in his good eye terrified me.

"My dog went missing again."

I'd never heard that tone in Ripley's voice before. So quiet. It made my stomach hot and liquid, the contents of my gut rose into my throat. Had Red Jackson caught Tyrus?

"You should have kept him chained," I cried. "It's not my fault your dog runs off. It's not Ezra's fault either."

"You know who found him? The soldiers, at the dead-zone border." Sweat ran down Ripley's face. It dropped onto me. I clamped my jaws tight to keep the vomit from coming up.

"Tyrus is dead," Ripley said.

My hand plunged into the thick mud, trying to dig my way out from underneath him. I couldn't breathe.

"Tyrus is dead." His voice rasped over me. He was crying. Ripley Powers crying.

"It was radiation poisoning. Doc Prentice cut him open. It's the law now when they find a dead animal. Did you know that? Four months after the accident. It's his fault." Ripley tossed his head toward Ezra, who lay unconscious, bleeding in the mud. "It's his fault."

I felt his hard weight crushing me, bruising my bones. I grabbed at fistfuls of mud, trying to get free.

"Get off," I yelled, twisting beneath him. "Get off me."

Ripley glared.

"I can't breathe!" I cried.

And then suddenly Ripley pitched forward. One moment he was rigid with fury. And the next he collapsed and rolled off of me. I couldn't figure out what was happening.

I sat up in the middle of the road, trembling. I fought to catch my breath. My eyes focused on Ezra, lying in the mud, blood pouring from his face.

I thought for a moment it'd been Ezra who'd saved me from Ripley. I saw now I was wrong.

Ezra couldn't have saved me from anyone.

It was Muncie.

Her muddied mask dangled around her neck. At her side, she held her backpack. The heavy backpack she'd used to smash over Ripley's head.

Ripley groaned.

A few yards away, Ezra tried rising to his feet, but he couldn't.

"Muncie, help me get Ezra to the house."

Muncie never even hesitated.

Ezra rose out of the mud between us, leaning on us as intently as he had once leaned on Gramp's canes.

The blood wouldn't stop streaming from his face.

Suddenly Caleb bounded up, and Shep, barking wildly. Shep had never jumped the fence before. And then Gran came, and Mrs. Trent.

They moved Ezra into the back bedroom and tried to halt the bleeding. It wouldn't stop.

"Bring me towels," Gran ordered.

I raced to the linen closet, my hands trembling.

Gran took the towels and hustled me out of Ezra's room. "You two girls get cleaned up," she said. "I'll take care of things in here. Muncie, don't let your parents see you in those bloody clothes."

Muncie led the way to the kitchen and opened the door, looking out toward the road. "I can't see Ripley anymore," she said. "Probably crawled back to his hole."

"I shouldn't have let him get to me."

"He'd been asking for it," Muncie said. "For as long as I've lived here, he's been asking for it."

"But look what I did to Ezra."

"Your grandmother will take care of Ezra."

She was talking to me like nothing had ever come between us.

We went into the bathroom and washed the worst of the dirt and blood off our hands and faces. "Come upstairs," I said. "I'll get you something clean to wear."

"Like your clothes really fit me."

"All right. We'll get something from Gran's room then."

We went into Gran's bedroom. I hardly ever went in there. It was a simple room, nearly bare but for a double bed, a chest of drawers, a wardrobe, and a straight-back chair. No rug. A plain brown blanket on the bed. The only decoration was a sepia picture, of Gramp as a baby.

I didn't know where to look for Gran's clothes, but I felt funny going through her drawers. I tried the wardrobe instead. It smelled nice, cedar.

The light from the window barely touched inside, so I opened the wardrobe door wider. I expected to find sweaters, or blankets, maybe old pants. I found none of those.

What I found in the wardrobe was a doll, nearly bald, dressed in pale blue overalls. Circles of elastic gathered the material around the ankles, tiny pink flowers dotted the shirt. The doll sat on the low wardrobe shelf.

My old doll.

I picked it up, brushed back the few honey-brown strands of its hair.

"Your grandmother plays with dolls?"

This was too private. I didn't want to talk about it at all. But it was time. It was time to talk to Muncie.

"It was my doll. When I was little. My mother gave it to me before she died."

"And you didn't know your grandmother had it all these years?" Muncie asked.

I shook my head. "I'd thrown it away."

Setting the doll back where I'd found her, I started to close the wardrobe door when Muncie stopped me. Reaching in, she pulled out an old photograph.

"Who's this?" she asked.

She handed me the snapshot.

A slim, unvarnished woman stood beside a man with dark eyes, a square jaw, muddy boots. He stared uncomfortably at the camera. The woman, her face turned sideways, smiled at a baby riding her hip. The sun slanted through a window behind them. The baby must have moved as the shutter clicked because her smile blurred in a line between the man and the woman, almost connecting them. The wall behind them had green-and-gold striped wallpaper.

I remembered this. I remembered not only the picture, I remembered the moment.

"That's my mother," I said, pointing to the thin woman. "And my father." I touched his white shirt, unbuttoned at the cuffs and the neck.

"And that's me." I touched the baby. "That's my crib. I used to sleep sometimes in the back bedroom."

I placed the photograph beside the doll, closed the wardrobe softly, and opened a dresser drawer.

"Here," I said, holding out a work shirt and a pair of pants. "She won't mind if you borrow these."

I went back across the kitchen, down the hall, and listened at Ezra's door. I heard Gran's voice talking calmly, slowly. She had things under control. Gran always had things under control.

Voices still rose and fell softly behind us as Muncie and I climbed to my room. We peeled off our muddy, blood-stained clothes. I didn't look away while Muncie undressed. I wanted to see her. I tried not to flinch when she watched me too.

At one point I thought I heard a truck idling, but Muncie's high-pitched voice chatted on. A numb exhaustion made everything slow, unreal.

I examined the pricker bush scratches down my arms and legs. They swelled in red striped welts. Some of the scratches still bled.

I stepped into my jeans and pulled a clean sweatshirt over my head. Mud caked my hair.

"I need to get this muck out and check on Ezra."

"Sure," Muncie said.

"Will you come with me?" I asked.

Muncie looked at me, a slow grin unfolding across her face.

"Thanks for the invitation, but I'd better get home. You know how my parents worry."

"Muncie?"

"Yeah?"

"Thank you."

Muncie grinned. I hadn't seen her face in a long time. She pushed her glasses up onto the bridge of her nose and rocked on her short legs down the stairs.

As I climbed down behind her, every muscle in my body clenched with pain.

"You better put your mask back on," I said at the kitchen door.

"It's full of mud," Muncie answered.

"Do you want me to walk you home?" I tried listening for sounds from Ezra's room, but I couldn't hear anything.

"No thanks," Muncie said.

As soon as she'd gone, I felt fear creeping up the steps of my spine. The house was too quiet.

I rushed to the back bedroom—no one was there! In the bathroom only towels drenched in blood.

I tore outside.

Gran's pickup was gone.

They'd left. They'd left me.

How could Gran leave me like that? How could she take Ezra away? Without even telling me.

I paced back and forth, from one end of the house to the other. Picking up all the bloodied towels, I dumped them in the tub and soaked them in cold water. Dragging myself out the door, I went through the motions of evening chores.

And when everything else was done, I tried chopping wood. To keep busy, to keep from thinking. But I had no strength left.

I put the axe down and sat on the broad stump, staring at the empty house.

Twenty-eight

I'd been out in the cold for hours. A deep chill radiated from the pit of my stomach. They'll be back any minute, any minute. But no headlights turned up the road, no truck clattered over the bridge and slogged up the hill through the mud.

A dog howled. That would be Tyrus. No. Not Tyrus. Tyrus was dead.

Caleb sat beside me. Bayley had run out, and somewhere in the dark he crept silently toward his dinner. Would he eat something radioactive the way Tyrus had? Would Bayley die too?

I heard footsteps coming from a long way, coming across the frozen mud. I didn't move off the stump. Just touched the handle of the axe. I wouldn't let Ripley near me again, never again.

Then I recognized the rhythm of the footsteps. Not Ripley. My hand relaxed.

Not Ripley.

Muncie.

"I'm over here," I called.

Muncie jumped.

"What are you doing outside?"

I told her that Ezra and Gran and Mrs. Trent were gone.

"He'll be okay," Muncie said. "You know he'll be okay."

But Muncie couldn't make a promise like that. Nobody could. I had seen Ezra on the edge of death, just as I'd seen Gramp, and my mother. Sometimes people let go. This time Ezra might let go.

Muncie steered me into the house. The stove had grown cold.

"I'm no good at building fires," Muncie said, poking a stick around in the ashes.

I got the kindling burning while Muncie warmed coffee on the electric stove.

"Drink this," she said, thrusting a cup laced with cream and maple syrup into my hands.

I couldn't drink. I couldn't sit still. It was as if something stalked me in that house. If I sat still it would catch me.

"I've got to get out of here," I said, leaving the coffee untouched.

"You want to come to my house?"

"No. Not there. Come with me."

I led Muncie into the tractor shed.

My hand moved over the equipment, over the smooth bodies, the hard seats. The cold burned my skin.

There was the radiation detector, hanging from the wall. And up on a ledge made by the timbers, the watches with their luminous dials silently, unceasingly emitted their traces of radiation.

Muncie listened to me as the whole story poured out. She listened, saying nothing.

I led her across the pasture, retracing in the dark the steps Ezra and I had taken his first day out. Muncie and I slid and struggled across the snow. "The walking's too hard for you," I said, watching Muncie strain to keep up with me.

"Everything's too hard," Muncie said.

I stopped in the middle of the field.

"What if he dies?"

"He was dying anyway," Muncie said. "A lot of them are going to die. The doctors said that months ago. Mrs. Haskins said it."

"He was not dying!" I screamed.

"He was. We're all dying, Nyle," said Muncie. "Haven't you figured that out yet? We all have to leave sometime."

I stared at Muncie in the moonlight. How did she know?

I had always thought I was so much stronger than her, smarter than her, better than her.

"Let's go back," I said. "You're shivering."

I adjusted my pace to Muncie's and we moved, slowly, two shadows under the night sky, shuffling across the treacherous ice.

Together we sat on the chopping block, shivering, waiting.

"Look, Nyle," Muncie said. "It won't do any good for us to get sick too. Why don't you go in and lay down awhile? Your grandmother will wake you when she gets back."

"What about you?"

"I can stay with you."

"Your parents will worry."

"They know where to find me."

I felt the violence of Muncie's shivers press against my side.

"Why didn't Gran tell me she was leaving? Why didn't she take me? Maybe I wanted to come too. Maybe I wanted to say good-bye. Just say good-bye."

"Your grandmother does things her way. Just like you, Nyle. You're both impossible."

I reached out and touched Muncie's arm. Headlights were slowing down at the road, slowing and turning up this way. I heard the whinny of a truck downshifting.

Muncie and I stood, waiting in the blinding headlights.

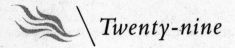 \ *Twenty-nine*

New leaves uncurled beneath the warm April sun. Gran's truck bounced along the frost-heaved roads. There was no money to fix them, no more road crews. The state couldn't afford road crews anymore.

I held a gift wrapped in marbled paper against my chest.

"This isn't going to be easy, Nyle," Gran warned.

"It's all Ripley's fault," I said bitterly.

Gran shook her head. "No, Nyle. The leukemia had already taken hold of Ezra before Ripley pounded him. That's what made him bleed like that, the leukemia, not Ripley. Cookshire caused this, not Ripley Powers. The radiation Ezra absorbed triggered the cancer, sped up its growth. In a way Ripley did Ezra a favor. Who knows how long Ezra would have waited to tell us he was sick?"

Gran found a space in visitor parking and we walked to the entrance of the hospital.

Inside, we stopped at the reception desk.

Ezra was in room 804. My nostrils constricted at the smell as we got off the elevator. The whole place gleamed with cleanliness, but an odor lurked underneath, an odor that made me want to turn and run.

I stole a glance into each room as we passed; patients sitting or lying in their sunlit beds. Some my age, some older, some younger. This was the cancer ward. It was full to capacity.

In room 804 the curtains were drawn. But I recognized Mrs. Trent, even in the dim light. She sat beside Ezra's bed, staring at the wall opposite her. She wore one of my dresses, and over it a sweater of Gran's.

Mrs. Trent looked up as we entered the room. She blinked, stared at us. Suddenly she stood, opening her arms. I went to her, like a lamb to a ewe. Her scent closed around me.

Ezra lay on the bed, eyes shut, a bandanna patterned like the American flag tight around his head. His large hands rested outside the sheets.

Stepping back, I stared down at the bed. This couldn't be Ezra. But there was the scar.

"Ezra," Mrs. Trent said.

Ezra's eyes opened partway. Tired eyes, the spark extinguished.

Gran extended a hand to Mrs. Trent. The two stepped out of the room.

I sat in the chair beside the bed.

"A present," I said, extending the package toward him. He was too weak to take it from me.

"Should I open it for you?" I asked.

I unwrapped the marbled paper. My hands shook. I made a mess of the wrappings.

The book inside was my copy of *Slake's Limbo*. I had inscribed it. *From Nyle to Ezra.*

I opened the book to the first page.

In every other room the curtains had been open. Not here. Here the curtains shut out all the warmth and hope of spring. It was impossible to read in the dim light.

I remembered the first time I'd read to Ezra. I felt so certain he would die in the back room, as Mama had, as Gramp had. Everything had changed since then, and yet nothing had changed.

I tried reading. Ezra's hand moved slowly, painfully across the great distance from the top of the sheet through the rail to my arm.

His hand wrapped weakly around my wrist, stopping me.

I swallowed hard. In the silence, I heard my heart shatter.

Ezra drifted in and out of sleep. I sat, making myself watch him. Letting myself feel the pain of losing, the pain of leaving.

A tube pumped oxygen into his nostrils. It cycled every few seconds. I counted. One. Two. Three. Four. Five. Six. Pump. One. Two. Three. Four. Five. Six.

"How you been, Shep?" Ezra's voice rasped in his throat. His words came out thick and sluggish.

I nodded. Made myself answer. "You're missing the lambs, Ezra. What kind of sheep farmer misses the lambs? It's the best part."

Silence again. I knew there must be sound outside this room. Life outside this room. Why couldn't I hear it?

"Been thinking," Ezra said. "Anne Frank."

I stopped him. "It's spring Ezra."

"Maybe," Ezra said. "Maybe—they'll remember me, too."

I couldn't tell him the world had already forgotten him.

"How's the radiation out there?"

"It's fine," I said. "Fine."

"Open the curtains," he whispered.

"What?"

I brought my ear close to his lips.

"Open the curtains."

The hand tightened on my wrist.

"But—"

"Nothing more to fear," he said.

I opened the curtains. He had a beautiful view of the Connecticut River. The sun fell across his bed, creating shadows and light through the room.

Ezra sighed. "I waited for you, Nyle."

"Well, I'm here now." I sat back down beside the bed, took his hand gently in my own. "Gran wouldn't let me come any sooner. She said it would be too much. I don't know whether she meant too much for you or too much for me—"

Ezra tried to laugh. Just a small sound.

"Can I do anything for you?"

Ezra shook his head. "Remember the night—Anne Frank? You read my letter?"

I nodded.

Ezra almost smiled. "Good."

His eyes stayed open, stayed on my face.

I bent over the rail. Gently I touched the bandanna with my fingertips.

"Take it off," he whispered.

Carefully I removed the bright bandanna, revealing soft
180/ wisps of hair, all that remained of Ezra's thick curls. I stroked
the fine bones of his skull. Then I touched the craggy eyes;
his bones felt so fragile, so close to the surface. I had always
wanted to touch his face. My fingers whispered over his
cheek, found the scar, stayed there.

Ezra's eyelids shut and he trembled. A hint of deep purple
showed beneath his lids.

"I'm tired," he said.

"I know."

"Nyle, I have to leave."

"I know that too, Ezra."

"You'll be okay?"

"Ayuh."

He nodded. A glistening in the corner of his eye. I
touched it with my finger, drank it into my skin.

With one of my hands curved under, one wrapped over
top, I surrounded his bony fingers with everything good
inside me.

He never opened his eyes again.

Gran and I walked back to the truck. We kept our own space.
Not daring to touch.

"Why?" I asked, hardly trusting my voice.

"Nyle," Gran said as she headed the truck back home. "I
don't know."

"But accidents happened before. They happened in
other places. Somebody knew."

"More people needed to know. More people know now.
Maybe enough people. Something will be done."

I thought about how at first everyone talked about the accident. But now, other news was more important, as if Cookshire had never happened. How could people forget?

Mrs. Haskins said all of us would be touched by it. And we were. Yet nothing changed.

"You really believe that?" I asked. "That something will be done?"

"Ayuh," Gran said. "But maybe, Nyle, you have to be the one to do it."

Mrs. Haskins had said our class should write letters. I didn't know what to say then. Would it make a difference if I wrote now?

"It's too late for Ezra," I said.

But it's not too late for the rest of us.

Back home we passed Shep, guarding the flock in the flat pasture along the main road.

"I'll get out here," I told Gran.

Uncle Lemmy stood inside the front pasture, surrounded by lambs. He looked fine up there, right at home. He, Aunt May, and Bethany had come to stay in the back bedroom. Bethany was getting better, slowly, slowly better.

Uncle Lemmy agreed to move in last month and help Gran with the spring work. The rest of my cousins had gone to stay with Uncle Lemmy's brothers.

Shep sat at attention as I walked up.

We'd trained him well.

I climbed over the fence, sank to my knees and buried my head in his side.

There was no more puppy smell to him. Only outdoor

smells, grass and pine, seeds and wind, and sheep, the oily, woolly smell of sheep.

Shep nuzzled my hands, my arms, my legs. He had found Ezra's scent on me. He searched, sniffing out every inch that had connected me to Ezra.

Kneeling, I held the enormous head against my chest. The sun blurred as spikes of light splashed off my lashes.

At the edge of the upper woodlot, Muncie appeared. She waved in silent greeting. Reaching out to her, I waved back.